6.00

Helen's Temper

© 2016 by TGS International, a wholly owned subsidiary of Christian Aid Ministries, Berlin, Ohio.

All rights reserved. No part of this book may be used, reproduced, or stored in any retrieval system, in any form or by any means, electronic or mechanical, without written permission from the publisher except for brief quotations embodied in critical articles and reviews.

ISBN: 978-1-943929-10-8

Cover and layout design: Kristi Yoder

Illustrations: Igor Kondratyuk

Second printing: October 2020

Printed in the USA

Published by:
TGS International
P.O. Box 355
Berlin, Ohio 44610 USA
Phone: 330-893-4828
Fax: 330-893-2305
www.tgsinternational.com

Helen's Temper

Originally published in London

by James Nisbet & Co.

21 Berners Street

1872

Mrs. George Gladstone

Table of Contents

1. Who Is Your Neighbor?........................... 7
2. To Seem and to Be 25
3. Louisa Goes to Sunday School............ 35
4. Practical Betty...................................... 49
5. Louisa Profits by Betty's Lesson 61
6. The Young Teacher 75
7. Helen Forgets Herself.......................... 87
8. Suffering Louisa................................... 99
9. The Two Friends 111
10. Grandfather's Present 121
11. Grandfather's Story 133
12. The End 145

Who Is Your Neighbor?

A group of children was gathered around their teacher one Sunday afternoon, and had just finished reading the parable of the Good Samaritan. Miss Herne then told them to close their Bibles, and began to ask some questions to see if her pupils understood what they had just read. She looked at Betty Smith, the youngest scholar in her class, and said, "Betty, can you tell me who is your neighbor?"

"Yes," replied Betty, without giving herself

HELEN'S TEMPER

time to think. "Mrs. Jones."

A general titter went around the class, and Betty's eldest sister Helen, who sat next to her, gave her an angry push with her elbow, and muttered, "How stupid you are."

"No, Betty is not stupid," said Miss Herne, who heard these words, "and she is right in one respect. We call the person who lives next door to us our neighbor.

"But before I ask any more questions, I wish you to listen, children, while I try to explain this parable to you in a few words. Christ tells us that a certain man was journeying from Jerusalem to Jericho. We are not told to what nation or rank of society he belonged, but he was probably a Jew. The road was dangerous and infested by robbers, who were always on the watch to attack travelers. The man was proceeding quietly on his way when some robbers came upon him. They tore his clothes off his back, wounded him grievously, and when they found nothing more was to be gotten out of him, they departed, leaving him half-dead.

"While he lay unconscious, a priest passed along. Perhaps he had come from performing the temple service at Jerusalem, and you would have thought that a man who had been worshipping God would have had pity on a sick and suffering one. But no; though the law of Moses commanded him to help those who were in trouble, he did not heed it. The moment that his eye fell on the wounded man, he crossed the road, and may have congratulated himself that he was not thus incapacitated. A Levite came next. He looked on the sufferer, perhaps even touched him to learn how much he was injured. But certainly, as his superior the priest had passed by on the other side, it was not his place to attend to the wounded man. So he crossed over the road and went on his way.

"Then came the Samaritan, who was one of a race that was despised and hated by the Jews. He was moved with deep compassion when he saw the wounded man, and thought to himself,

'How can I help him?' He walked up to the stranger's side, not to look at him out of curiosity, but to decide how best he could assist him. He raised him up gently in his arms, bound up his wounds as well as he was able, and set him on his own beast, leading him carefully along the road until he came to an inn. He remained that night with the invalid, and in the morning, when he departed, he left money in the landlord's hands, and said, 'Take care of him; and whatsoever thou spendest more, when I come again I will repay thee.' All this the Samaritan did out of love, and not because he expected to be paid for his kindness.

"Our Saviour then turned to the lawyer and asked him this question, 'Which now of these three was neighbor to him that fell among thieves?' The lawyer replied, 'He that showed mercy.' Now, Betty, can you tell me who is your neighbor?"

"I can," volunteered Helen. "And so can I," echoed several voices.

WHO IS YOUR NEIGHBOR?

"No, children, I do not want any of you to answer. I am asking Betty, and wish her to think before she answers my question."

Betty hesitated for a moment before she replied, "Anyone who helps us in trouble."

"Yes, Betty, you are right. And now, my dear children, you may act the part of good Samaritans. None of you are too young. Christ is our Good Samaritan. He showed mercy to us when we were dead in trespasses and sins, and as He loves us, so ought we to love our neighbors."

The children listened attentively to Miss Herne's explanations, and several of them answered the questions she asked as though they understood the whole bearing of her teaching, particularly Helen Smith, who thought before she replied, while her sister Betty was so quick she scarcely allowed herself time to consider.

As Miss Herne went home that Sunday afternoon, she said to herself, "How different the two sisters Helen and Betty are! Helen is only one year older than Betty, and yet far more thoughtful. She acts twice her age, and she is so industrious too. Ah, if all my pupils were like Helen Smith, what pleasure I should find in my Sunday class." How true it is that God sees not as we do. He looks at the heart, while we judge by the outward conduct, and therefore often form very wrong opinions of others.

Helen and her sister Betty walked home from school together, and as they passed through a narrow street, they met a little girl who looked terrified, and seemed in great distress. Her dress was torn, her boots were full of holes, and her bonnet was so small it would not come on to her head, but fell down on her shoulders and left her pale though clean face unprotected. Her eyes were full of tears, which she tried to hide, and she appeared anxious to shrink away from the two neatly dressed girls, for she was lame, and her back was so crooked that only the hardhearted could look on her without feeling pity for her infirmities.

Betty Smith was soft and tender by nature, and she could not walk on without speaking to the child and trying to serve her.

"What is the matter with you, little girl?" she asked quickly, without asking her sister's permission, which perhaps she would not have granted.

"I have lost my way," answered the lame child sadly. "I cannot find the yard where I live, and I am very tired."

"Where do you live?" asked Helen sharply.

"In King's Yard, on the right hand side of Henry Street," replied the child, looking very much frightened.

"Henry Street? You are a long way from there," said Helen roughly. "You must turn around to the left of the first lamppost, and ask your way again. It is easy enough to find, if you are not stupid. You ought not to go about alone if you don't know your road. There, don't cry. No one will touch a child like you." And Helen glanced consciously at her own much more tidy dress, and then at the miserable object in front of her.

The lame child tried to force back her tears, and her sorrowful "Thank you, miss" went straight to Betty's heart. "I will go part of the way with you, little girl," she said. "At any rate, I will put you on the right road, one that will bring you directly into Henry Street. So come along and take my hand."

"What nonsense, Betty," said Helen. "You need not show her the way. If she is silly enough to cry, instead of minding my directions, she must suffer for it. She must be a beggar's child, or she would not wear such shabby clothes. Come along quickly; we shall be home late as it is."

Betty did not heed her sister's words. "You go on without me, Helen," she said. "I shall not be long. I will be as quick as I can, and mother will not be angry if I am home at five o'clock. Tell her where I have gone to, unless, Helen, you will come with us."

"No, certainly not," replied Helen, tossing her

head up. "I am not so fond of going out of my way. You had better come home, Betty. The child will do very well without your help."

Betty shook her head, and remained firm to her first resolution. So one sister went home, and the other took the stranger's hand and led her into the right road. As the children walked along, they began to chat, and the lame child told Betty that she had lived only for a short time in King's Yard, and rarely walked out in the streets by herself, because she was so crooked that the boys sometimes laughed at her, and that was the reason why she knew so little about the neighborhood.

"Have you always been lame?" asked Betty.

"Since I was a baby. My mother fell down with me in her arms, and my back was so much hurt it has never gotten well again, but grows out, more and more, every year, and the doctor says he can do me no good."

"Oh dear! Oh dear!" said compassionate Betty. "That is very sad. How hard it must be to bear."

"Not so very hard," replied the lame child, brightening up a little. "I should not mind it much, if I could do anything like other children. But I cannot play, for I soon get tired, and my mother says that I shall never be strong enough to be a servant. And even if I could work, no lady would have such a crooked maid to wait on her."

"Then why should you not be a dressmaker, like my mother? She makes dresses for grand ladies, and I shall do the same when I am old enough," said Betty. "Can your mother make dresses?"

"No, I don't think she can, though she works very neatly," replied the lame child. "She is a washerwoman, and her hands get too rough for very fine work now. Besides, she generally comes home so tired that she is fit for nothing in the evening. But we could not live if she did not earn money in this way," added the child, sorrowfully.

"Is your father dead, then?" asked Betty.

"No, but so ill that he cannot work. He had an accident some months ago, and has been laid aside for a long time. We were once much better off than we are now, for we had our own little house, and such a pretty garden, and I had a corner of ground all to myself. I used to plant it with seeds every year, and there was a beautiful white rose tree in the middle that had so many roses on it, and numbers of buds. I loved it very much, but I had to leave it behind. I often think of it, and fancy how sweetly it smelled when I am sitting in our dark little rooms, where there are no green trees to look at, and no roses to bloom."

"Have you any sisters?"

"Yes, I have two sisters, both of them are younger than I am. I take care of them when my mother goes out washing."

"Where have you been to this afternoon?" asked Betty, who seemed to think she had a right to question her new friend. Was she not the little girl's protector?

"I have only been for a walk," replied the lame child. "My mother said it would do me good, for I have had such a bad headache all day."

"Then you never go to Sunday school?"

"No."

"Where does your mother go on Sunday?"

"Nowhere. She is so glad to have the day at home, for she has so much to do. Sometimes she puts my sisters to bed while she washes their flannel petticoats; sometimes she washes her own clothes or scrubs the floors of our rooms. We often have a great treat on Sunday: if Mother has had plenty of work, and can afford it, she buys a little bit of meat for dinner, and we do so enjoy it."

"But do you not know," said Betty, "that it is very wrong to work on Sunday? No one ought to wash clothes or scrub floors on God's day. We ought to read our Bibles, and go to Sunday school, and to church, and think about good things. Has no one ever told you so before?"

"Yes," said the lame child slowly, "I have

heard all that before. I know rich people go to church and read their Bibles, but poor people have no time to be good."

"Why not?" said Betty. "Have not the poor souls as well as the rich?"

"Yes, I believe so," answered the child, absently, as if it were a matter that did not much interest her.

"It is so," said Betty. "And my teacher always tells me that our souls are precious in the sight of God, and that we ought to think more about them than our bodies."

"But no one does that," replied the lame child.

"Oh, yes, many people do. And if we are careless, we ought not to be. How can we go to heaven if we don't read our Bibles, which tell us how to get there?"

The lame child sighed, and looked very weary as Betty continued. "Our teacher says that if we love Jesus, we will love Sunday school, going to church, and hearing about God. She says we should value Sunday, because we can rest and learn about the Saviour. Do you love Jesus?" she added softly.

"No," said the lame child, astonished at this question. "I know so little about Jesus."

"Why don't you come to Sunday school, then, and hear more about Him? Miss Herne tells us about Jesus every Sunday. What He did in this world—making the blind to see, the deaf to hear, the dumb to speak, and how He healed lame people like you."

"I wish He would heal me, and take away my crooked back, and make me like other girls," said the child.

"He would have healed you, if you had lived in those days and believed in His teaching," answered Betty, "and He will know if it is good for you. Miss Herne always says that if we ask God for anything He will grant it if it is good for us, and that He loves us and cares for us, and is our best friend. Will you not come to Sunday school, and hear our teacher tell you all this so much better than I can?"

"I think I will, if—"

"If what?" asked Betty, eagerly.

"If I can manage to get tidier clothes. But then that is not all."

"What else?" said Betty.

"I am so lame, the girls will laugh at me."

"No," said Betty indignantly, "they would not be so cruel as that, and they dare not before Miss Herne. If your clothes are clean, what does it matter if they are old? If you will go with me, I will come and fetch you next Sunday."

"Is it very far to the school?"

"Not far from where you live, because we can take a shortcut."

"I will ask my mother," said the lame girl, "and if you will let me go with you, I shall not mind so much. Here is Henry Street. Thank you for coming with me; it is very kind of you. That is my mother in front of us, she will wonder where I have been to. Will you speak to her?"

"No, I had rather not," replied Betty. "Another

day I shall like to come and see you both, and your little sisters too."

Betty was a timid child, and feared the mother would thank her for taking care of her lame daughter. She took a hurried leave of her new friend, first asking what her name was.

"Louisa Hall," replied her companion.

If Louisa had heard Miss Herne explain the parable of the Good Samaritan on that Sunday afternoon, she would have been able to answer the question, "Who is your neighbor?"

To Seem and to Be

Helen was not long walking home, and found an unexpected guest in her mother's parlor. Mr. Holt, her grandfather, lived two miles away, and had come to have tea with his daughter, Mrs. Smith, who had been left a widow four years before our story opens. Helen sprang forward to kiss her grandfather, and then turned around to answer her mother's question, "Where is Betty?"

"She will soon be here, Mother. As we came

from school, we met a beggar girl who said she had lost her way. I fancy she was pretending a little, but Betty was silly enough to believe her, and said right away that she would take her home."

"I would call that kindness on Betty's part," said Mr. Holt, seriously, for Helen's tone and manner did not please her grandfather.

"Well, perhaps it was," replied Helen. "But the little girl was very lame, and so poor that I would have been ashamed to be seen with her, but Betty does not mind. I believe she would go with a chimney sweep if she were asked."

"Be quiet, Helen," said her mother. "Your tongue runs too quickly. Take away your hat and cloak, for I am going to get tea ready."

"Helen grows fast," remarked Mrs. Smith to her father, when the door had closed on her daughter.

"Yes," replied Mr. Holt, "she is taller, but I am not sure that she grows wiser."

"She has a great many faults. Helen is too

fond of dress, and very much afraid of being laughed at by her friends. But she is apt and clever at her books, and she learns her lessons while Betty is thinking about hers," answered Mrs. Smith.

"Learning is not the chief thing in life, daughter," said Mr. Holt gravely.

"No, my dear Father, I know it is not. And I often think that though Betty is not as clever as Helen, she is more kind and generous, ready to help everyone, and to do good to those who need her assistance as far as she is able. I only wish she loved her books more."

Saying these words, Mrs. Smith left the room and went into the kitchen to see if the kettle boiled. She sent Helen to her grandfather while she prepared for the meal and cut the bread and butter. Mr. Holt questioned his grandchild about the lessons that Miss Herne had taught her that Sunday afternoon, and Helen gave a good account of all she had learned. She was able to remember the substance of what her teacher had said, and spoke so sensibly that her grandfather felt she understood the parable of the Good Samaritan, and he only hoped she would apply her knowledge to her daily life.

"Are you going to be like the Good Samaritan," asked the old man, "and help all who need your assistance?"

Helen did not much care about answering this question. Her conscience told her that though she was able to remember all she had heard and learned in Sunday school because she had a good memory, she really did not care to apply it to herself. She did not care about other people; whether they were happy or miserable, it was no matter to her. In fact, she knew that at heart she was much more like the priest and Levite who passed by on the other side. But Helen was so accustomed to stifle her conscience that she answered with apparent interest, "I am afraid, dear Grandfather, I cannot do much good while I am so young. When I am older I shall try to help others."

"No one is too young to be useful, Helen," answered her grandfather. "There are many neighborly acts that you may perform for others. You may lend your books and toys at school to your companions. You may speak kindly, and encourage those who are not as clever at learning as yourself. You may be tender to your mother, and try to save her anxiety and trouble. And if you meet a ragged girl in the street who has lost her way, and is crying, you may take her hand, sympathize with her sorrow, and lead her to her mother. I thought you would remember these words of Scripture, 'He that is faithful in that which is least, is faithful also in much; and he that is unjust in the least, is unjust also in much.' As you are now, my child, so you will be when you grow older, and therefore it is important you should have right ideas and right feelings while you are young. I am glad that you know so much about the Scriptures, Helen, but I wish that you would try and carry God's words into all your actions."

It was a great relief to Helen to hear her sister's step at this moment. Betty came in looking very heated, for she had walked home quickly.

"How are you, little woman?" asked her grandfather kindly. "I hear you have been home with a poor lame child who lost her way."

Betty was almost too much out of breath to answer directly, but gave her grandfather a bright smile, and, after a few moments, replied, "I did not know you were here, Grandfather. She was such a poor little girl, and so unhappy that I felt I could not leave her. She was smaller than I am, not quite as old, and so shy and frightened. She would never have found her way home if I had not been with her."

"You were right to take care of her," said Mr. Holt. "Always be useful, Betty, in little things. Was the child so very poor?"

"Oh, yes," replied Betty. "She had such old boots on, and a ragged cloak. And, Grandfather, the boys laugh at her in the streets, and point at her because she is deformed and lame. Is it not wicked? She had a very clean face, and said her father and mother were once better off, and she had a beautiful white rose tree that she left behind in a little garden of her own, when they lived in the country."

By degrees Betty told her grandfather the whole of the conversation that had passed between herself and Louisa, and closed by saying, "And she has promised me that she will go with us next Sunday to Sunday school."

With us, thought Helen. *I am not going with that nasty, shabby child. Why, Alice Howes and Mary Eames will fancy she is related to me. I will scold Betty well when I get her alone.*

While these thoughts were passing through Helen's mind, she was smiling graciously at her grandfather, and seemingly interested in listening to her sister's account.

"Now, Betty," said Mr. Holt, "Helen has told me what chapter you read at school this

TO SEEM AND TO BE

afternoon. Did you understand it?"

"Yes, Grandfather. Miss Herne explained it so clearly to us that I quite understood it."

"I think you must have, Betty. So much so that you were able to act the part of neighbor to little Louisa. Is it not so?"

Mrs. Smith summoned the trio to the kitchen at this moment, so that Betty only nodded her answer to her grandfather's question.

The little family gathered around the table, and during tea-time Mr. Holt told his daughter and grandchildren the story of a young girl who lived near to him, and was there lying at the point of death. "And though she is only twelve," added the old man, "just your age, Betty, she believes in Jesus, and rests entirely upon Him, and trusts in Him alone for salvation."

Betty listened attentively, and Helen seemed to pay great heed to her grandfather's words, for she sat very still, but really her thoughts were far away. She was picturing to herself her friend Mary Eames's new bonnet and cloak, and wondering whether she could persuade her mother to buy her a new bonnet and cloak before next Sunday, and she would have them even nicer than Mary's, if possible. She determined she would coax her mother, though she was not sure of success.

Mr. Holt did not remain long after tea was over, for he had some distance to walk home. Helen was rather glad to be rid of her grandfather's presence and his lectures, while Betty said to herself, "How nicely Grandfather talks, and he is so good too. Everyone loves him. I hope I shall grow up like him."

Louisa Goes to Sunday School

Betty thought many times about Louisa, and wondered whether she would go to Sunday school, and how the girls would behave to her. The little maiden determined to protect her new friend, and if all Betty's prayers to God during that week had been printed, several of them would have been found to contain such petitions as these:

O God, help poor Louisa to love thee, and don't let the girls laugh at her if she comes to

HELEN'S TEMPER

Sunday school, and grant that she may love Jesus. And, if it is good for her, please make her crooked back straight, and let her grow up as strong as I am, and be able to play about.

When Sunday came, Betty dressed herself earlier than usual in order to have plenty of time to walk to King's Yard and fetch Louisa. Helen tried hard to induce her not to go, and was cross because her sister said she would not break her word, and when Betty endeavored to persuade Helen to accompany her, the latter said angrily, "I am not going to associate with a half-naked, crooked child. Think, Betty, what Alice Howes and Mary Eames will say when they see you come in with that ragged little girl. I shall be quite ashamed of you."

"Helen, do not speak so wickedly," answered her sister. "Poor Louisa did not make herself."

"Be sensible, Betty," replied Helen, "and come with me, and then I will not laugh at your deformed friend anymore. You are welcome to have her all to yourself, only don't let the girls at Sunday school see you bring in a beggar."

Helen's cruel words did not influence Betty. She started off to fulfil her promise in spite of her sister's anger, and walked so quickly that she soon reached King's Yard. It was a small court, and the houses were closely packed together. Betty was thankful she did not live there, and was not surprised that Louisa longed after trees and flowers. She soon found No. 3, and knocked at the door. It was quickly opened by Louisa, who had been watching for Betty to come, and she had been looking out of the window dressed and ready for the last half hour. She wore the old bonnet that was so much too small, the same threadbare cloak, but her boots were neatly mended, and she had on a well-patched but clean print dress. Certainly it was much too long for her, as it was her mother's best gown, and Louisa found it was difficult to walk in, but she tried to gather it around her carefully, and its many folds somewhat hid her deformity.

Betty and Louisa shook hands cordially; they were very glad to meet again.

"So your mother will let you go," were Betty's first words. "How glad I am."

Mrs. Hall came to the door before the children started off, and thanked Betty for taking care of her child a week ago. She asked some questions about Sunday school, and told Betty that Louisa had not forgotten last Sunday's conversation, nor her new friend, nor the promise Betty had made that she would take her to Sunday school, and that Louisa had watched the weather anxiously lest it should rain and she be compelled to remain at home, as she so easily took cold.

Mrs. Hall had evidently been well educated, and seen better days. Her face was worn by care, and deep lines could be traced on her brow. Her eyes were sad and weary, and seemed to say, "I have had a hard life." Two little children, untidily dressed, were hiding behind an old coat that hung upon a peg on the door, and kept peeping out at their visitor, and disappearing again when they met her glance.

Betty could not remain talking for very long. She was anxious to be early enough to secure a quiet corner for Louisa near to Miss Herne, but the child was too lame to hurry along the road, so the first hymn had been given out before they reached the school. This gave Betty no opportunity of interesting her teacher on the little cripple's behalf, nor was she able to put Louisa into the snug corner, so she whispered to her companion, "Sit down by my side."

Louisa obeyed, but blushed rosy red when she saw so many eyes fixed on her. Some looked out of curiosity, others contemptuously, while a few cast glances full of pity on her wasted and deformed figure. She had a pretty face, and deep blue eyes that filled with tears out of very shyness. Alice Howes and Mary Eames were the two who looked scornfully at poor Louisa, and, though they were forbidden to speak in school, Alice bent down to Mary and said, in a voice that was loud enough to reach Helen's ear, "Is that a cousin of Betty's?"

"No," answered Helen angrily, drawing herself up proudly at the mere thought of such a thing. *I knew how it would be,* she said to herself, while her lips were singing the solemn words of the hymn. *I knew how it would be if Betty brought that ragged child here. I was*

sure the girls would laugh at her. It's not right of Betty to expose me to all this.

Betty and Louisa looked over the same hymn book and Bible, and as Louisa could not read well, Betty pointed to the words, so that she was able to follow each syllable. Miss Herne explained every point so clearly that Louisa learned many new things that first afternoon that she attended Sunday school. The children read the story of the Saviour walking on the Sea of Galilee, and Louisa thought she must be dreaming, she seemed in such a new world. She had never heard these words explained before; in fact, she rarely read the Bible. Her parents were not in the habit of gathering their children around them on Sunday to enjoy the words of God's own Book, and her pale face brightened more and more as Miss Herne made clear to her pupils many simple truths, and told them that if they lived without Christ, they would be just like the disciples who were rowing against wind and tide, but that if they loved the Saviour, rest and peace would follow them everywhere.

Those were glad words for the little deformed one to hear. She had hitherto shrunk from observation, and sometimes longed to die, because she was so unlike other children, and could not play. Rest and peace in Christ came like sweet music to her weary spirit, and she thought that if it were really true that Christ loved every one, she would not be forgotten.

Louisa's home was not a happy one. Her father and mother were kind to their children, but usually so full of trouble and anxiety that the days were spent in striving to find means to procure daily bread. The parents shed many bitter tears when they saw Louisa and her sisters going to bed night after night hungry, or sometimes only half satisfied with a morsel of dry bread and cup of cold water, or one potato, which was all they had to give them. When Louisa's sisters were born, Mr. and Mrs. Hall did not live in London. They had a pretty house in the country, and the husband earned a goodly sum every week. Unfortunately, he fell in with evil companions, and the cottage was gradually stripped of all its comforts, and the wife and children began to learn the meaning of the word "want." Mr. Hall made many promises of amendment, which he broke when the first temptation came. At last he determined to go to some other place, and, hearing of a situation in London, he moved his family to that city. His wife was glad to make any sacrifice to ensure a change and improvement in her husband's habits, and she was thankful that the move had been made, as for many months after they came to London their prospects brightened.

Then a terrible misfortune happened to Mr. Hall. He fell from a high ladder, and was taken up from the pavement much bruised, and conveyed to a hospital. After weeks of extreme pain and suffering, he was pronounced to be so far recovered as to be able to return home. He was so weak that he could not work, and each day grew more feeble. He might have improved with good air and plenty of nourishment, but how was that to be procured when he only had his wife's earnings to depend upon, and three children requiring daily bread? The family removed from their more comfortable lodgings to King's Yard, and Louisa's mother worked very hard to maintain her husband and family. She procured regular washing, and was well paid for her work; but though she practiced the strictest economy, she could scarcely afford to buy meat once a week, and often there was no coal to burn on a winter's night. Thus it was no wonder that Louisa's cloak was shabby, and her boots full of holes, for Mrs. Hall had to depend on charity for her children's clothes. The money she gained barely provided food and firing, much less garments.

Betty introduced Louisa to Miss Herne after school was over, and the latter welcomed her new pupil kindly and encouraged her to come regularly to Sunday school.

The two children walked home together. Betty bravely passed her sister Helen and her smart friends, leading Louisa by the hand. Though she heard scoffing, laughter, and mocking words, she did not appear to heed them, but talked pleasantly to Louisa, and would not leave her until they reached King's Yard. Louisa wanted Betty to come in, but the latter said, "No, I must go home, dear, and I am sure you will want to tell your mother all about Sunday school."

Louisa went in with a cheerful smile on her face. The hour spent at the school had made her happy. She forgot the contemptuous glances, and only remembered what Miss Herne had said, her kind look of welcome, and her explanation of God's Word. She had hitherto heard her father groan and moan over his accident, and inability to work. She had never before listened to any words that bid her hope and trust in Jesus through all the trials of life.

HELEN'S TEMPER

Louisa told her mother every detail that she could remember. There was a strong bond of love that linked these two together, for Mrs. Hall always considered that she was to blame for letting her child fall out of her arms, though it was a pure accident. But, mother-like, she thought it was due to lack of care on her part.

"I was able to learn the text, Mother," said Louisa. "It was so short. 'Come unto me all ye that labour and are heavy laden, and I will give you rest.' Is not that pretty, Mother? And our teacher spoke so beautifully of rest in Christ. After the girls were gone, and only Betty and I left behind, I went and spoke to her, and just as we were saying goodbye, she whispered in my ear, 'There is rest for you, little one, though you have so much sorrow to bear. Do not forget this afternoon's text, but be brave, my child, and come to Jesus.' Were they not nice words, Mother? They made me so quiet-like."

"Yes, Louisa, they are beautiful words."

And Mrs. Hall sighed as she said so. She

remembered that before she had grown so poor, she had thought more about Christ, but lately she had been too tired to pray. The poor tempest-tossed woman sat down, and, covering her face with her hands, burst into tears.

Chapter 4

Practical Betty

Betty had to undergo a certain amount of persecution from Helen, Alice, and Mary, about her new friend. They even declared that they would go to Miss Herne, and tell her that they were not going to associate with a dirty beggar girl. But this threat did not affect Betty. She remembered her teacher would uphold the lame girl's coming to the school. Helen did not dare to express her contempt for Louisa openly, for she felt sure her mother and grandfather would be angry if they knew how much she disliked the little cripple. So she mocked and jeered at Betty when they were alone, and even struck her sister in anger one day when she refused to promise not to take Louisa to Sunday school again. Betty was often sorely tempted to tell her mother of Helen, but the child disliked to give pain to her parent, so she resolved to remain silent as long as Helen only laughed and mocked, but did not openly attack Louisa. At the same time Betty told Helen, with great determination, that if she showed any unkindness to Louisa, she would inform Mother and Grandfather, and Helen knew that her sister would keep her word.

Betty had a hymn book that had been her companion for many years, and she had long desired to have a new one. She counted her halfpence and found she had enough to make her purchase, for she needed only one shilling. So she determined to give her well-worn book to Louisa, and buy another for herself. When

Wednesday afternoon came, Mrs. Smith and Helen went out shopping together, and Betty resolved that she would take her present to her new friend, first asking her mother's consent. Mrs. Smith readily granted it, and said, "You may take a few apples with you, Betty. I have picked out some rosy-cheeked ones; they will please Louisa and her sisters."

Betty could not resist giving her mother a hearty kiss. She then packed away the apples in her own little basket, and started off to see Louisa, whom she found at home with her sisters. Her father had gone to the hospital, and her mother was at her washing. Betty had not been inside the room before, and now saw that it was small and uncomfortable. The corners were black with dust and dirt, the walls were damp and colorless, and the furniture was old and rickety. Louisa sat on a broken chair, with her knitting, while her sisters rolled on the ground, with grinning faces and uncombed hair. But the trio looked happy and content;

they were talking over a story that Louisa had just finished. The lame girl was delighted to see her new friend. She put the best chair forward for her to sit upon, and she evidently thought that Betty's clean frock and tidy appearance would not be improved by a sojourn in the dirty room, for she said, blushingly and as if in apology, "Mother went out very early, and had no time to clean the room, and the last few nights she has been so tired that she was obliged to go to bed directly after she came home."

"Can you not help your mother to keep the room clean?" asked Betty. "It would be a good thing for her to rest every evening after her hard work."

"I do not know," replied Louisa sorrowfully, "for I never tried."

"I think you can if you try," said Betty kindly. "You are nearly as big as I am, and I often sweep out the room, take the ashes out of the grate, and clean it up. My mother says I do it well."

"But your rooms are better than ours,"

answered Louisa, looking around at the narrow four walls. "I only wish we had a different home."

"I know our rooms are larger," said Betty, "but they will not keep themselves clean any more than yours will. My mother says every place is worth keeping clean however small and humble it may be, and we ought to make it look as nice as we can. I know what I would do if I were you, Louisa. I would scrub the room before my mother came home, and then I would fill the pail with clean water and see if I could not wash some of the dirt and dust away from the corners. And, if you like, I will show you how to begin."

Betty was active at home, and could do the work of a much older person. Her mother often said she did not know what she should do without her. But it was a difficult matter to make Louisa believe she could clean a room. She had been taught only to knit, for Mrs. Hall thought that her lame daughter had no strength to spare for hard work. In her love and thoughtfulness for Louisa, she forgot how much happier her child's life would be if she felt she were assisting her mother, and thus not shut out from being useful to someone. Louisa had been content to sit still and allow her mother to do the house work, without reflecting in how many ways she might lighten her heavy burden.

Betty's words made Louisa think seriously, and after a pause of a few minutes, she turned to her friend and said, "Do you really mean that you will help me?"

"Of course I do, this very minute," answered practical Betty, taking off her cloak and hat. Then she brought the chairs and Louisa's sisters into the bedroom that opened out of the room which served for Louisa to sleep in at night, and for the family to live in during the day. The young ones were easily managed; Betty's activity was so new to them that they were content to stand in the doorway and watch her movements.

"I'll tell you what I'll do," said Betty. "I'll scrub the floor, and you shall clean the walls, because, just at first, it won't do for you to begin with such hard work."

Louisa found a scrubbing brush which had evidently seen great service, and a ragged flannel, with a lump of common yellow soap, while Betty went down to the pump in the yard, returning with her pail full of water by the time Louisa had routed these articles out of the cupboard.

Betty set to work in good earnest, as if she knew what she was about, and had scrubbed many floors before. Louisa tried to rub some of the dirt off the paper, and the cobwebs from the corners, and then washed the paint on the doors and the windows. Then she cleaned the glass through which the sun had not been able to penetrate for many a long day, and Louisa's sisters clapped their hands with delight when they saw the panes of glass looking so bright

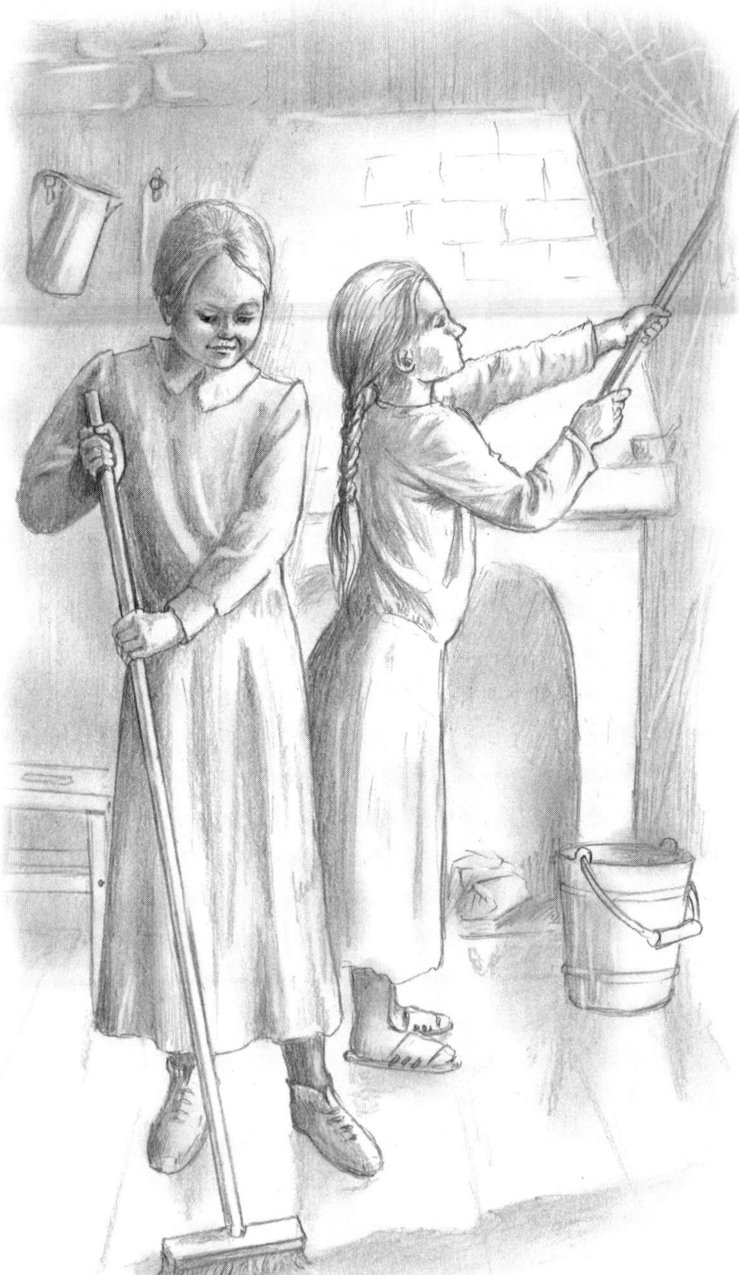

and clean. Betty looked up from her scrubbing and said, "Mind you never flatten your noses against the windows again. Then they will stay clean longer."

The girls worked on, heedless of time, until the room was clean. It was only half the size of Betty's mother's parlor, and she had finished the floor in an hour. The day was windy and the sun shone brightly, and sun and wind helped to dry the floor quickly. At the end of two hours the old chairs and rickety table were back in their proper places, and Betty had tried to make Louisa's sisters useful, and had showed them how to dust, and made them put the furniture where it usually stood. After this, Betty, Louisa, and the two little girls sat down to rest. Betty's face was hot, and Louisa felt very tired, but there was so much pleasure mixed with the weariness that no one regretted it.

"Betty, you have made me so happy," said Louisa. "I shall try to be more useful every day. And if I can't be like other children and play, I shall still be able to help Mother, and make her home look brighter when she comes in tired, and Father too will be so pleased. I wonder why I never tried before."

"Because no one put it into your head," replied Betty. "If Mother hadn't taught me, and showed me, and made me useful, I wouldn't have done it myself. I dare say your mother didn't teach you out of kindness, because she thought it would hurt your back. I hope she won't be angry with me for letting you work."

"Oh, no," answered Louisa. "I shall tell her how happy I am to be useful. My days will go so much faster."

"And there's another thing you must learn to do—that is, to comb and dress your sisters." Then Betty told the little ones a story about tidy children and encouraged them to help themselves. After that they talked about Sunday school, and Betty asked Louisa not to mind if Helen and her friends said unkind words, or mocked and laughed at her. Later on, Betty brought out her hymn book, and lastly, she divided the rosy-cheeked apples.

The three hours Betty had to stay passed rapidly. The children liked listening, and their visitor had so much to say. The apples elicited a scream of delight from Louisa and her sisters; they so seldom tasted fruit that they valued them the more. Betty was preparing to go home when the children asked her to teach them how to sing a hymn. So she sat down again, and was busily engaged in making Louisa and her sisters repeat the words of a verse after her, when the door opened and Mr. Hall entered the room. He did not appear to notice anyone or anything, but sank down on an old chair in the corner, evidently much exhausted. Betty saw that he was very weak, for his hands trembled, and his face looked so pale.

"I must go now," said Betty, who feared that the invalid would not care to have a stranger in the room. "Goodbye, dears," and with a kind look of sympathy at the suffering man, she left King's Yard.

As Betty walked towards her more comfortable home, she puzzled her little brain to know how best to help Louisa's father get better and obtain employment.

These questions were rather beyond her, so she determined to refer them to her mother, who she knew would be ready to aid her with her advice and sympathy.

Chapter 5

Louisa Profits by Betty's Lesson

When Betty reached home, she prepared the tea, and cut the bread and butter. Then she swept up the hearth, put the kettle on the fire, and made all in readiness for her mother and Helen's return. Mrs. Smith came home alone, and thus Betty had a good opportunity of talking to her mother, for Helen had been invited to spend the evening at a neighbor's house.

Mrs. Smith listened kindly and attentively

to all that Betty said, and was deeply interested in her account of little Louisa's home, and the scrubbing and cleaning up of the room. She promised to try and procure her better clothes for Sunday school, and told Betty she might invite Louisa to spend the afternoon on the next half-holiday. "It will be a treat for her," said kind Mrs. Smith, "and then I shall be able to see what clothes I had better give her. You have some old things, Betty, and I suppose they will fit your new friend, as you tell me she is about your own size and age."

"Yes, Mother," replied the little maiden eagerly, "and as Louisa is shorter than I am, you will be able to cut off the parts that are much worn."

"I understand, then, Miss Betty, that you mean me to make all the alterations for your friend. Well, I am quite ready to employ my fingers on the little cripple's behalf."

Betty thought Wednesday afternoon was very long in coming. Louisa was there exactly at two o'clock, the hour that was fixed by Mrs. Smith. Her face looked very clean, her hair was tidily parted, and she had evidently tried to make her ragged dress look better by running up the largest holes. It was a festive day for her. Mrs. Smith busied herself with shortening a frock of Betty's for her, and fitted her with an old cloak of Helen's, and a straw bonnet that she had outgrown.

"Oh, Betty," said Louisa, "how kind your mother is to me. I have not had such beautiful clothes since I was very young. The girls will not laugh at me anymore for being badly dressed."

Betty was not so sure about that, but she did not express her thoughts, and answered her friend cheerily, "I shall be quite proud of you on Sunday, Louisa. Teacher will hardly know you for the same, you will look so different."

Betty's remark was true. When the neatly attired child presented herself in King's Yard that evening, her own mother did not recognize

HELEN'S TEMPER

her at first, and was going to answer the question that her daughter put in a feigned voice, when the truth dawned upon her, and she called out, "Why, it's our Louisa!" There was plenty of rejoicing then. The little ones stroked their sister's cloak admiringly, and her father and mother said so many kind things about her good looks that Louisa quite forgot for the moment that she was lame, and had often felt life so wearisome. She was radiant with happiness, and exclaimed in her glee, "Oh, Mother, it's so nice to think of going to Sunday school, dressed like other girls. I only wish some kind friend would be as good to my sisters as Mrs. Smith has been to me."

When the excitement of the new clothes had partially subsided, Louisa brought out a basket of food Mrs. Smith had given her, and the family gathered around the old table and enjoyed the good supper sent to them. Even Mr. and Mrs. Hall forgot their hard life for a while, and joined in the merry chat that went on between Louisa and her sisters.

The only person who was not pleased at the attention that Louisa received was Helen, who hated and was jealous of her, and almost disliked her sister for being kind to the lame girl. Louisa was poor and deformed, and Helen was ashamed of her acquaintance. If Louisa had been rich and pretty, it would have been different, for Helen loved fine rich people. She was too selfish to be glad at the gleam of brightness that had come into Louisa's life since she had known Betty, and too proud in spirit to rejoice over the change that Betty was gradually bringing into this hitherto miserable home in King's Yard. Helen liked to be number one, and did not care to be interfered with. Therefore when Louisa spent the afternoon at her mother's house, the naughty girl had not concealed her dislike to the cripple, but had treated her with such evident contempt that her mother ordered her to bed at tea-time. This occurrence did not tend to improve Helen's feelings toward Louisa, and she raged in her room against the "beggar girl" who had been the cause of her receiving this punishment.

When Betty and her mother were alone that evening, Mrs. Smith asked her youngest daughter many questions, and learned with sadness how cruelly Helen behaved to Louisa every Sunday. Betty did not aggravate her sister's conduct; rather, she tried to excuse it by saying, "Mother, Louisa goes with me, and we do not mind when we are together. It's really Alice and Mary's fault. If Helen were not led by them, she would act differently."

"But, Betty," replied her mother, "Helen is old enough to know the right and the wrong, and it is very wicked of her to make fun of a child because she is poor and lame. I must talk to her grandfather about it."

If Mrs. Smith could have read all the bitterness that Helen felt against poor Louisa, she would have shuddered, for her daughter, as she lay in bed, was muttering, "How I shall pay off that little child!"

Louisa had profited by Betty's lesson, and had managed to keep the bedroom and sitting room tolerably clean since the day that Betty had scrubbed them, and had advised her to be useful, and set her to brush and dust. She thought she would never forget her weary mother's look of pleasure, nor her words of thanks, when she entered the room on the evening of that day. Though Louisa could not work long at a time, by doing a little each day she found she could keep the home in better order. Her sisters were gradually becoming useful. The elder of them, Sarah, managed to scrub the floor tolerably after she had practiced with the old brush and flannel a few times, for Louisa found her weak back would not allow her to do such hard work. But she was at hand to encourage Sarah, and ready to praise every effort the child made.

Louisa had effected considerable reformation in several points; her sisters always looked much more tidy and clean, and she mended the holes in their ragged dresses, and tried to teach them to read. In fact, every Sunday she came home from the school with fresh strength to work, and ready to put forth some new effort to help her parents and sisters. Louisa was learning more about Jesus every week, and she tried to remember that He was looking down and smiling on her all the day long, and she knew His blessing would follow every attempt she made to promote the happiness and well-being of those who were nearest and dearest to her. She did not forget on Monday what she had learned on Sunday, but tried to act out through the six days the lesson she had learned on the first day of the week.

A month passed before Betty went to see Louisa again. During that time the little girls had met every Sunday, and Louisa had spent two Wednesday afternoons at Mrs. Smith's house. But now Betty had presents to take to her friends, and therefore set off immediately after dinner in the direction of King's Yard. Her mother had given her a piece of muslin to make a doll's frock of. Betty did not tear it up, for she thought it might be applied to a more useful purpose. She remembered the bare window in Mrs. Hall's room, and was sure it would be much improved if it had a white curtain, which would hang over the ugly wall, and prevent everyone from seeing into the room so plainly. Betty felt she was almost too old to play with a doll, and so she determined to consult her mother, and if she approved, to take her large wax doll, and give it to Louisa's sisters.

Mrs. Smith agreed with Betty that curtains would make Mrs. Hall's room look more furnished, and she thought the muslin would be so well applied that she offered to give her daughter enough material to make a second curtain to match, and also consented that dolly should find a new home in King's Yard. Betty started out heavily laden. She took a box of clothes, the collection of many years' standing, which contained garments for the doll, and muslin for the curtains. When she entered Louisa's

LOUISA PROFITS BY BETTY'S LESSON

home, she was astonished to see the change her perseverance had wrought. The table and chairs looked clean, the fireplace bright, the walls were pasted with new paper, and a picture hung on one side of the room.

Louisa's father had done this. When he saw that his children were trying hard to improve the aspect of the hitherto dirty home, he determined to do his part in helping them.

Mr. Hall was in his usual corner by the fire, leaning his head on his hand, when Betty entered. But the latter lost her nervousness in her delight, and exclaimed, "Oh, Louisa, how pretty your room looks!"

"My father did it," said her friend joyfully. "Is he not very clever?"

"Yes," Betty replied. Then the children discussed the question of the curtains, and Mr. Hall entered with interest into the conversation, and smiled an assent when Betty asked him to help nail them up, as she was not tall enough to reach so high.

Betty, Louisa, and her father soon nailed up the muslin securely. Then, after admiring their work, another nail was put in on one side of the window, and a second nail on the other side for the curtains to be tied to loosely, so that they should not blow about too much. The children thought that nothing ever improved a room so much as these muslin curtains. "What will Mother say when she comes?" was the cry. "They do look so nice."

The enjoyment of the afternoon was not yet exhausted, for Betty had to give her doll. A child who has never had a doll, or remembers the first birthday one that was given, can understand the pleasure of little Sarah Hall and her sister when Betty unpacked her doll. Louisa enjoyed looking at it as much as the younger ones, and even Mr. Hall admired the flaxen hair, pink cheeks, and wax arms and legs. The dresses and hats were considered so beautiful, and the fashionable cloak that Mrs. Smith had made for Betty out of an old bit of velvet, and the muslin frock, and silk dress—all were so lovely to these children, who had so few toys, and so little enjoyment in life.

Betty thought, as she lay down to sleep that evening, it was very pleasant to make people happy, and she was glad that the rooms where Louisa lived were cleaner. "And I am so pleased," said the little maiden to herself, "that I helped Louisa to be useful."

Betty dreamed all night long, and her dreams were bright. At first she was teaching a number of children to scrub, and the brushes seemed to be made of gold, and the water shone like silver. Suddenly the children disappeared, and Betty found herself in a beautiful world, and a man clothed in bright garments was calling and beckoning to her. He said, "Come up here, little girl, up to this glorious world, because you tried to teach and help others, and loved Jesus."

Just as Betty made one step forward, she awoke, and found it was morning, and she felt sorry she had not slept a little longer, so that she could have known where she was going to. "It was only a dream," she said. "I'm so sorry. And now it's time to get up, and I cannot find out what that pretty place, which seemed so splendid in the distance, was like."

CHAPTER 6

The Young Teacher

*S*everal months passed by, during which time Betty and Louisa's acquaintance had ripened into strong attachment. In fact, Betty wondered what she had done without Louisa, and the latter hardly understood how she had managed to live so long without her warm-hearted friend. Poor Louisa did not grow stronger in health, and sometimes suffered so much pain in her back that she had to lie still for hours. But, in spite of her suffering, she managed never to miss

Sunday school. Her sisters had learned to be useful, and kept the rooms tidy and clean, thus sparing Louisa's strength, while she in return was able to teach them all that she had ever learned in former days, when her mother had sufficient money to pay for her schooling.

One Sunday afternoon Betty noticed that her friend looked sad, and as soon as school was over, she asked Louisa what was the matter.

"My father is very ill indeed, and the hospital doctor says that he cannot recover," answered Louisa.

"Does he stay in bed all day?" Betty asked.

"No, he gets up after breakfast and sits in the old armchair; but he is very thin, and his cough troubles him constantly."

"Sometimes men who are very ill do get better," said Betty. "Perhaps your father will recover."

Louisa shook her head, and Betty continued, "It will be very hard to part with him, but if he can never get better here, he will soon be well in heaven."

"Yes, if he loves Jesus," answered Louisa. "But he does not seem to care about Him. A neighbor said yesterday to Mother that if Father died, he would go to the dear Saviour, and Mother said that she could not bear to part with him, she loved him so much."

Louisa's tears choked further utterance, so she hurried away from her friend, for she wished to be home early.

"Mother," said Betty, running into Mrs. Smith's parlor, "poor Mr. Hall is very ill, and Louisa thinks he will never be better again."

"I am afraid she will be right, Betty," replied her mother, "for he has been ill so long. It is a great comfort that Mrs. Hall is able to keep a home for him. I will call and see him as soon as I can, but I fear this week I have too much work on hand. I shall not have a moment to spare."

"May I go tomorrow?" asked Betty. "We have an extra half-holiday at school."

"Yes, you may, Betty, and you shall take a nice piece of roast beef to Mr. Hall, for his poor wife can have no time to cook for her husband, and I fear she has no money to buy nourishing things."

The next afternoon Betty started off to see Louisa, and to hear how her father had passed the night. She carried a basket well filled with provisions, and a bottle of wine for the invalid.

Mr. Hall was alone. Louisa had gone to the hospital to fetch some medicine, and taken her little sisters with her.

He looked very ill. Betty went up to his side and spoke kindly to him, and then she unpacked her basket, and tried to tempt him to eat. "It is very nice," said Betty. "You had better try a slice of beef. Mother thinks it will make you stronger. I will soon find a plate for you."

Betty went to the cupboard and fetched a plate and knife, cut some thin slices of beef, poured out a glass of water, and persuaded the sick man to eat. The invalid seemed to enjoy a few mouthfuls, and then a violent fit of coughing came on, which almost frightened Betty. When it was over, he said, "Oh this dreadful cough, I shall never lose it."

Betty wanted to cheer him, so she answered, "Yes, you will lose it when you are in heaven."

Mr. Hall looked astonished. "But Betty," he said presently, "everyone who dies does not go to heaven."

"Only those who do not love Jesus are shut out," replied the child, in some alarm.

"Can all go to heaven who love Jesus?"

"Yes," answered Betty, and then she thought for a moment, and said, "Jesus Christ is the way through which you may go to heaven. He died on the cross to save us, and if we love Him, and try to be like Him, we shall go and live with Him when we die."

"Does Jesus save those who have never served Him when they were young?" asked Mr. Hall.

"Oh, yes," answered Betty earnestly. "Teacher says it is never too late to seek Jesus, and that He came to save the worst of sinners, and

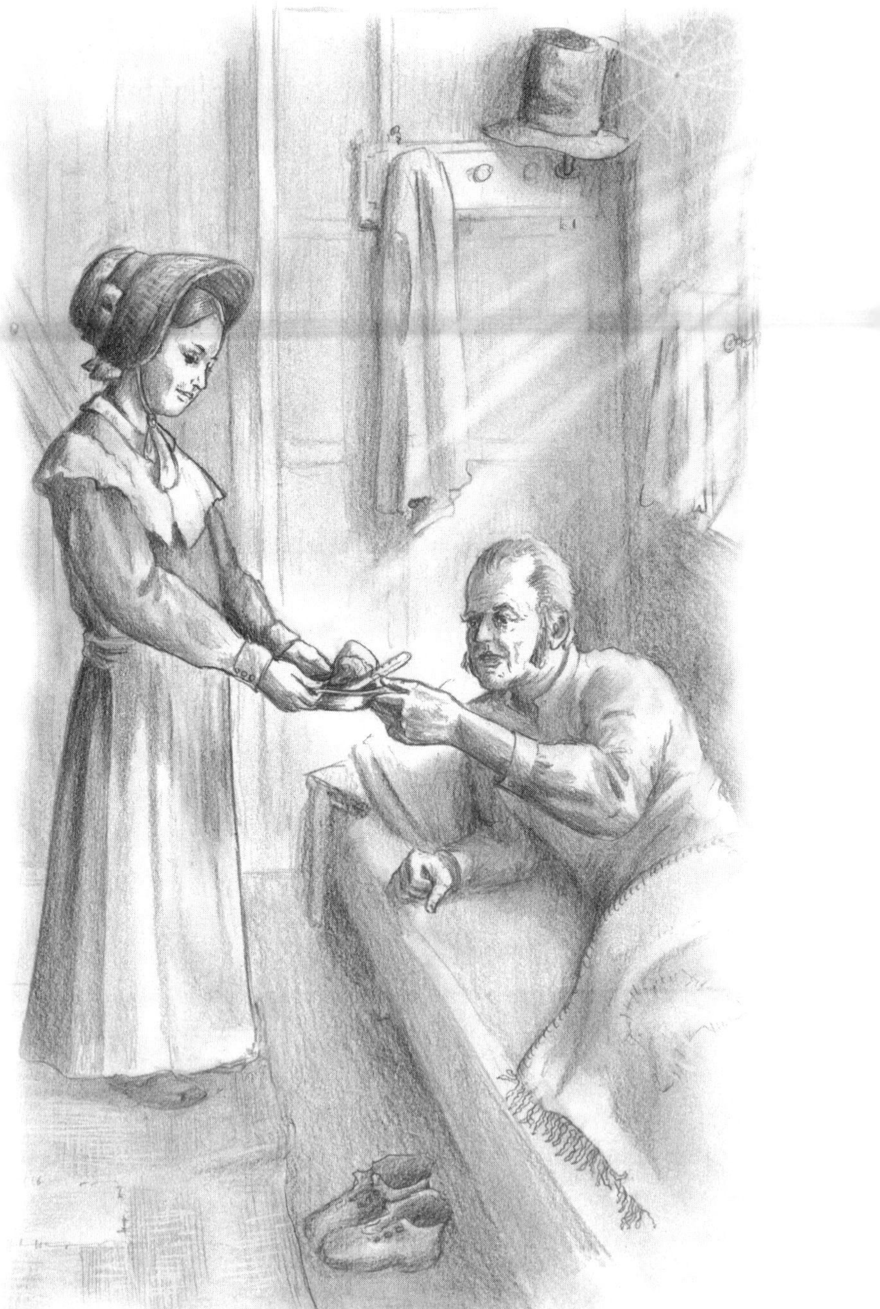

invites all to come to Him."

"Then you think Jesus will let me come to Him, though I am so old?"

"Yes, that He will," said Betty. "But don't put off coming to the Saviour any longer. If you love Him, you won't mind so much about your cough. At least, if it hurts you very much, you will think of what the dear Saviour suffered when He died for us."

"Did He suffer much?"

"Yes, don't you know the chapters in the Bible that tell us all about Jesus being crucified?"

"I used to read the Bible," said Mr. Hall, "but I'm ashamed to say I have not opened it for nearly twenty years."

"Then no wonder you are so sad," answered Betty.

"What has my not reading the Bible to do with my being sad?"

"Why this," said Betty. "If people feel miserable, and do not love Jesus, they have no one to talk to. But if you love Jesus, and are ill and wretched, you can go and tell Him all about it."

"Then you are sure that God hears prayer?"

"Oh, yes," replied Betty. "God has promised to hear us, and Jesus says if we ask anything in His name God will give it."

Betty's simple words of truth found their way into Mr. Hall's heart. He had been uneasy for some weeks past, and yet too proud to receive the teaching of his daughter. After his little visitor had left him, he thought over the conversation, and said to himself, "Jesus came to save sinners. He will save me, though I have been deaf to the Gospel for so long."

When Louisa returned from the hospital, her father asked her to read to him the story of the crucifixion. That evening the sick man prayed as he had never prayed before, and began to live a new life—one of faith and trust in the finished work of the Saviour.

A few days later, Betty, accompanied by her mother, paid another visit to Mr. Hall. When Mrs. Smith saw him, she hoped that he might yet recover, and determined that he should consult a new doctor, who was considered very skilled, and had lately come into the neighborhood. The kind woman promised to find the money, and went with Mr. Hall to hear Dr. Brown's opinion of his case. The doctor gave every expectation of the poor man's recovery, and Mrs. Smith returned to King's Yard with the invalid, and brought such good news to his downhearted wife that she hoped on again.

"You must remember, my friends," said Mrs. Smith before she took leave of Mr. and Mrs. Hall, "that God rules over all, and life and death are in His hands."

A few days later, Betty ran home from King's Yard in high glee. "Oh, Mother," said she, "Mr. Hall is so much better, and Dr. Brown thinks he will be able to do some light work in a month, and says he will employ him in carrying out his medicine as soon as he is strong enough, and that the walking about will do him good. Mr. Hall says he owes his recovery to you, after

God, for he thinks it is the nice food you have sent him that has helped him to get well."

"I am very glad, Betty, you have brought good news."

"Louisa is teaching her father to read and write better, for Mr. Hall says he left school when he was very young. It seems so funny for a great man to be learning like a child."

"I admire Mr. Hall for improving himself, Betty. No one need be ashamed of trying to gain knowledge, however late in life."

"No," said Betty, "but I never thought, Mother, that a grown-up man would have patience to learn."

"My child, Mr. Hall is learning in many ways just now. He is trying to find out the true source of happiness and contentment, and he is beginning to honor his Saviour."

"Yes, Mother, and Louisa says he hardly ever uses a bad word now, and is improving so fast in reading and writing that he will soon leave her behind."

"You seem very glad about all this, Betty," said Mrs. Smith.

"Yes, indeed I am, Mother. And Mr. and Mrs. Hall say that when Dr. Brown gives his permission, they will go to church on Sundays. Louisa's father says he has not been inside a church for many years. But why are you smiling?"

"Because you are so happy, Betty. What great things have come out of your taking Louisa by the hand, and showing her the way home."

"Yes, Mother, she would never have gone to Sunday school if I had not met her in the streets crying. Her father might have died if he had not seen Dr. Brown. Louisa and her sisters would have worn rags always. Now better days will come for them, I hope."

Betty had spoken so quickly, she stopped out of breath, and her mother patted her cheek tenderly, and said, "After all, dear, it is our heavenly Father who has been watching over Mr. Hall and his family."

Chapter 7

Helen Forgets Herself

During all this time we have not forgotten Helen Smith, and now must speak particularly about her, and tell our readers how she had been passing her time. Unfortunately, in some respects, her former friends had been her greatest tormentors, for Helen had quarreled with Alice Howes and Mary Eames. They were bad girls at heart, though they could sit and look so good at Sunday school. It was to be deplored that they went to the same day school as Helen and

Betty, and were in the same class as the former. They had quickly discovered that Louisa was clad in Helen's outgrown garments, and finding that she was teased by their scoffing words, they persisted in calling the lame girl "Helen's cousin," and never met her without asking her "how much she sold her old clothes for?"

Helen might easily have disarmed her adversaries had she kept her temper and befriended the poor little cripple. Instead of that, she was annoyed at being laughed at, jealous of the attention her mother showed Louisa, and angry at having been punished for her contemptuous behavior towards her mother's guest on that afternoon when Louisa was intensely enjoying Mrs. Smith's great kindness, and her first invitation out to tea since she had been so very poor. Added to this, her grandfather had spoken seriously to her, and scolded her for being so cruel to one who was so heavily afflicted, and badly off, as poor little Louisa. He contrasted Helen's comfortable home with

Louisa's miserable one, and asked her how she dare act thus to the poor deformed child whom God loved in spite of her poverty and lameness.

Helen might have become friendlier had she been far away from Alice and Mary, but every day the old sore was re-opened, and something said about Louisa that made her angry and jealous again.

No one ventured to touch the lame girl with Betty to stand by her. Alice, Mary, and Helen were too much afraid, but they tried to make Louisa very uncomfortable by staring at her. The latter took care to keep to her true friend's side, and on the rare occasions that Betty and she did not meet and walk to Sunday school together, Louisa managed to be in her place early, so as to avoid meeting Helen, Alice, or Mary. At length Helen grew so irritable over the perpetual blister that her friends applied to her that she visited her ill temper on her mother and Betty. She became so unpleasant that her mother reproved her many times, and thought it would be better to remove her to another school. Mrs. Smith had decided on taking this step when she heard, to her great satisfaction, that Alice Howes would leave the neighborhood with her parents, and that Mary Eames was going into service when the quarter ended. It would be only one month to its completion, so Mrs. Smith determined to make no change, and spoke again to her daughter. But though Helen seemed contrite for the moment, she did not display more friendship for the poor cripple and chosen companion of her sister Betty.

It was some weeks after Mr. Hall had recovered from his severe illness, and was living in Dr. Brown's service, that Helen and Louisa met face to face in a narrow court. Helen was in an unusually bad temper, for she had been wrangling with Alice and Mary. When the latter had seen how angry Helen had become, she had drawn a shilling out of her pocket, and holding it up high, called out, "I will give you this, Helen Smith, for your last old pair of stockings. You may as well sell them to me as to your grand cousin, Louisa Hall, who lives up two pair of stairs, at No. 3 King's Yard."

These words had been said on the playground, and Helen, furious at the attention they excited, struck Mary. The consequence of this was that she had to bear tenfold more harassment from the schoolchildren, and at length the governess, hearing the noise, interfered, and having dispersed her pupils, set Helen a long lesson to learn for the next day. We have said Helen and Louisa met face to face in a narrow court, before the former's passion had exhausted itself. The moment that her eyes fell on Louisa, a wicked spirit within seemed to say, "Here is that beggar who has caused you so much trouble—pay her off!"

Helen looked up and down the court; no one was to be seen. Louisa, who was always afraid of Helen, would have passed her with a little curtsy, when the latter came up to her side and said, in a low clear voice, "I hate you,

you nasty, deformed, ugly child. You have brought me nothing but trouble. You come to my mother with long stories to make her give you food. You pretend to be good to Betty, and all for what you can get. Go along with you, or I shall strike you, for I detest you so much." Saying these words, Helen gave Louisa a quick push, and passed her. She was not prepared for what followed. Poor Louisa, who was never strong on her feet, and had grown much weaker of late, reeled on one side, her head struck against a sharp stone, and she lay on the ground pale and motionless.

Helen was terrified, she knew not whether Louisa was dead or stunned, and being a thorough coward at heart, she ran up the court as hard and fast as her legs would carry her, and did not slacken her pace until within a short distance of her home. By the time she reached her mother's door she had nearly recovered her breath, and she went upstairs to her bedroom, and tried to still her beating heart. She

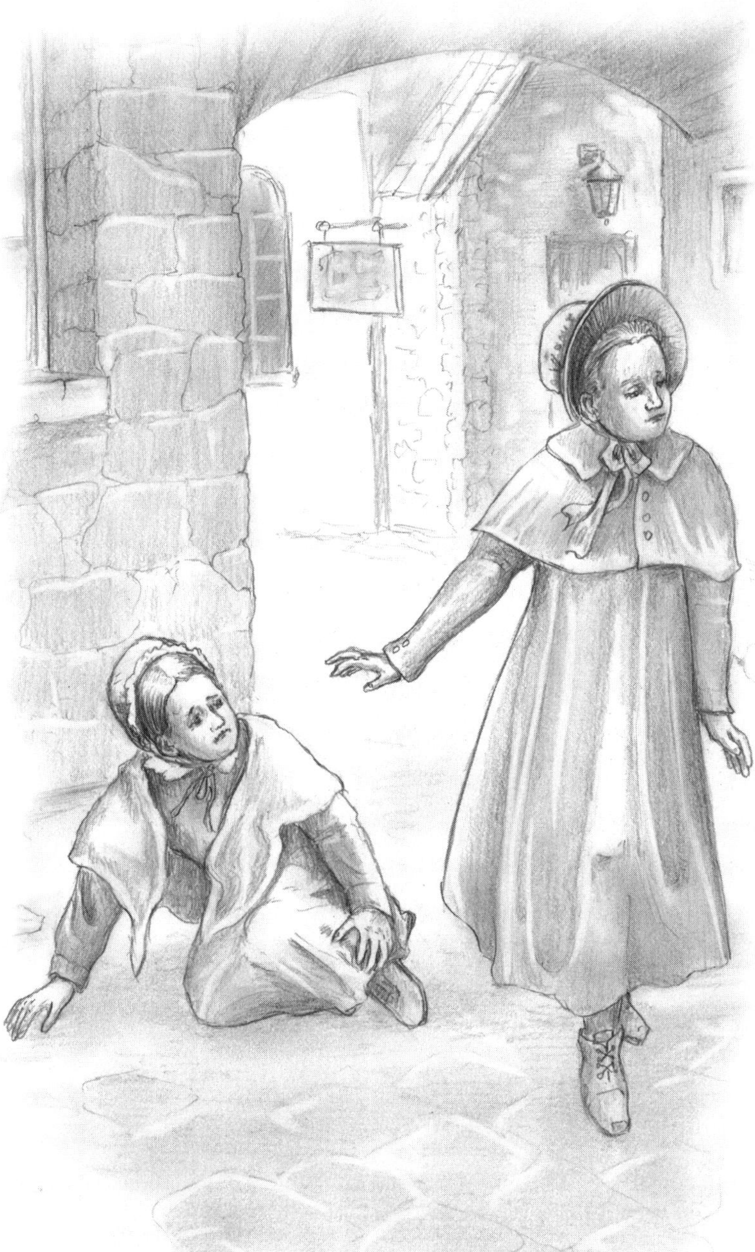

wished she had not left Louisa, but supposing she were dead it would be better for her not to tell anyone she had pushed her. *If Louisa lives, will she tell?* thought Helen. *Suppose she does; my word is as good as hers any day, and no one will suspect me of being a liar. There are plenty of ways of accounting for a fall. Louisa may have stumbled, everyone knows how weak she is, or she may have had a fit in the street. I had better keep quiet, and I will go down and help Mother to work, and no one will know that I met Louisa on my way home.*

Helen's fear was lest her friends should discover how wicked she had been. She cared not for the knowledge that her Father in heaven had, of every thought that passed through her heart that afternoon, before and since she had seen Louisa.

Helen, having smoothed her hair and washed her hands, went to the work room where her mother and Betty were sitting. The latter was helping to finish a dress that must be sent home in the evening, and had not been to school that day, having awoken with a bad headache in the morning.

"Mother, I have come to help you," said Helen. "I made haste home from school, for I knew you were busy."

Mrs. Smith looked at her daughter, astonished. She was so little accustomed to hear Helen volunteer her services. Her excuse was usually that she had lessons to be learned, or some fancy work that had need of finishing.

"Thank you, Helen. I have promised this dress tonight, and I shall be glad if you will take two breadths of the skirt to run together," said her mother, hoping this was the beginning of a better state of things. Helen's fingers were soon busily engaged, but if anyone had watched her face it would have been seen that she was startled by every sound, and kept changing color. A knock was heard presently at the door, and though it was only the milkman, she trembled. Then a neighbor came in for a few moments, and Helen dreaded lest she should speak of Louisa, or say that a lame child had been found lying hurt or dead in the court. Conscience began to make her uncomfortable, she was filled with dread fears, and her anxiety grew as night drew on.

Helen had never neglected her prayers to God, though she often knelt down and said words while her heart was wandering far away, but the habit was so strong that she felt uneasy when she threw herself on her bed without asking God to take care of her. But she dared not pray. What could she pray for? She could not ask God to pardon her when she intended to deceive her mother, and had already told her one falsehood, and did not mean to shrink from many lies if they were necessary to keep her secret. She thought she could pray if she knew how Louisa was. She wished she had kept her temper, but, after all, Alice and Mary, particularly the latter, were more to blame than herself. It was their wicked teasing that made her cross. But supposing Lousia were to die, would she be punished? Helen shuddered, for now, in the silence of the night, she could not get away from herself. Her sins stood before her, and she was obliged to think about them. One moment she tried to justify her conduct, and the next her wickedness rose up in all its enormity. She tossed from side to side on her little bed, and did not sleep until morning dawned, and then she dreamed she was being carried away from her mother's side, and was taken to prison for killing a lame girl.

Helen awoke screaming, and her cries brought her mother to her bedside to know what ailed her. Helen kept her secret, and tried to laugh away her mother's looks of anxiety. She was glad when school time came, for at any rate she would have less leisure for thinking. Though she knew the girls would tease her about what had passed the day before, she preferred their scoffing words rather than a state of inaction. Helen was more afraid of herself just then than of any living being, and it was the reproaches of her own conscience she longed to flee from.

CHAPTER 8

Suffering Louisa

On a clean bed, in a small room in King's Yard, lay a suffering child, so flushed and feverish, we hardly recognize pale little Louisa Hall. Money had been more plentiful since Mr. Hall had been able to work, and Mrs. Hall had hired a third room for her children, and lately purchased a small bed, so that Louisa might have the comfort of it, and not be obliged to sleep with her sisters. Betty had taught Louisa many things—there were all the elements of good in the latter before, and she needed only to be shown the way to Jesus to profit by the teaching of His Gospel. Since Mr. Hall's recovery, peace and rest seemed to have come to this family, and brighter days were in store for them, they hoped. Louisa's sisters had attended a free school regularly for the last four weeks, and Louisa was her mother's right hand at home, as far as her strength would allow her to work.

The previous evening sorrow overshadowed the home in King's Yard, for Louisa had been found lying unconscious in a narrow court. She had been sent by her mother to the grocer's, who lived in an open street not far from the spot where she appeared to have fallen. A good woman happened to pass who knew the deformed child. She lifted her up tenderly in her arms, and carried her home. Louisa had not been conscious all night, and her mother had not left her bedside for a moment. She had wandered in her mind a great deal, and Mrs.

Hall was puzzled to understand the meaning of the words which she repeated over and over so often.

"Betty, dear, I do not love you for what I can get, but for what you have taught me. Why does Helen hate me? Betty, Betty, I would not wrong you—save me from Helen!"

When the world began to move again, Mrs. Hall determined to send for their kind friend, Dr. Brown, whom she knew would come to them, for he had ever been such a true helper since he had known them. She awoke her husband, and before long he was rapping at Dr. Brown's door. It was early morning, and several hours before he usually began his duties in the surgery.

In the meantime, Louisa's consciousness returned. "Mother, where am I?" she asked.

"At home, dearest. You have been ill, and fell down in the street."

Louisa thought for a moment before she remembered all, and then she covered her face with her hands, and burst into tears.

"What is it, my darling?" asked her mother. "Never mind, we shall soon get you well again."

"Mother, I fancy I shall not be better any more. I have such a pain here," pointing to her side. "Why should I want to live? I am a cripple, and shall have no more pain to suffer in heaven."

"Oh, Louisa, I cannot lose you. My child, you are my right hand. Just as our lives are growing brighter, it would be too hard to lose you."

"As Jesus wills," replied the child, wearily closing her eyes, as if she had no more strength for further conversation.

Dr. Brown shook his head when he saw the invalid. "She has had a severe shock," he said. "Now, little one, tell me all you remember about your fall. How did it happen?"

"I fell, doctor. I am very weak, you know, and lately have been feeling as if I could hardly walk. I think my head must have knocked against something."

"What made you fall? Were you pushed down?"

"I can't talk any more, please, doctor," answered the child, sobbing bitterly. "Please, please, don't make me."

Dr. Brown did not press more questions on Louisa, lest he agitate her further, and after giving a few directions, he left King's Yard. *There is something behind this that she won't tell,* he thought as he walked home.

Towards afternoon, Louisa revived considerably, and her mother's heart grew lighter, for Dr. Brown had said no bone was broken. *And why should not Louisa get well?* she asked herself.

"Mother, I should so like to see Betty," said Louisa. "She does not know that I am ill, or she would have come to see me, I am sure. I want to talk to her alone, please. You'll not mind, Mother. I want to ask her so many questions, you know. Betty and I tell one another all our secrets. Oh, Mother, how much we owe her! She showed me first that Jesus would love me

though I was so crooked, and she made me understand that I might help you if I would try, even though I was so weak. And she talked to Father and made him believe he was not too great a sinner to be saved. I want to see Betty very much. Kiss me, dear Mother, and I will try and sleep. And will you ask Mrs. Smith to let Betty come back with you, and ask her to stay here until the evening? You know it is Wednesday half-holiday, and she will be at home. And, Mother, if you see Helen, tell her I sent my love."

Mrs. Hall found Mrs. Smith at home, and Helen and Betty were sitting working by her side. Helen would have run anywhere rather than hear what Mrs. Hall had to say, and yet she seemed spellbound. She wanted to know if Louisa were living or dead. She had spent a wretched day, not daring to seem anxious and ask questions about Louisa, in case suspicion should rest on her. Yet she longed to know something about the lame girl. Her mind had been wandering far from her lessons, and she had been severely reprimanded by her teacher. She returned home directly after school, wishing to avoid her companions, lest they should have heard of Louisa's misfortune, for she was afraid she could not command her countenance if any bad news were reported, and applied herself to her needle. It was a relief to employ her fingers rapidly, but now the dreaded moment had arrived. She must hear the truth and learn whether Louisa was dead, or, if alive, whether she had charged Helen Smith with that fatal push which seemed to produce such dire results. Oh, the agony of those moments between Mrs. Hall entering the room and declaring why she had come!

The poor woman looked very weary, and had evidently been shedding bitter tears. "Betty, I have come for you," she said, trying to speak calmly. "Louisa is very ill and wants to see you."

Then she was not dead. Helen breathed more freely.

"Louisa ill!" exclaimed Betty and her mother together. "What is the matter with her?"

"I hardly know," said Mrs. Hall. "She was found lying unconscious in a narrow court. I had sent her to the grocer's, and whether she had not strength to walk, or had a fit, or what, I cannot say, and Dr. Brown does not seem to know. She was unconscious all night, but towards morning became sensible. The doctor looked grave, and told me to keep her very quiet, for he is sure she must have had a great shock. She cries out for Betty, and I promised to take her back with me if you can spare her for half an hour, for I am sure Louisa must not talk to her for a longer time than that."

Then she had not told. Helen breathed again, but she thought, *What can Louisa have to say to Betty, unless she wants to complain of me?* After all, she would not be safe until she heard what Betty had to report about her visit. Poor Helen could get no rest. She had at least an hour to wait before Betty would have time to go to and return from King's Yard.

Betty soon put on her bonnet, and she and Mrs. Hall were nearly halfway up the street when the latter stopped suddenly and said, "Oh, Betty, excuse me for a moment; I must go back and give Louisa's message to Miss Helen. I promised not to forget it." And, without waiting for a reply, she ran back, and putting her head in at the parlor door, said, "Miss Helen,

I nearly forgot to give Louisa's message to you, and I know she will ask me if I have remembered it. She said, 'Mother, if you see Helen, tell her I send my love.'"

Was not this heaping coals of fire on an enemy's head? Helen looked very red, and was glad that Mrs. Hall did not wait for an answer, and that her mother was called away at the same moment by a neighbor. Helen's conscience did not allow her much peace, and yet she felt more comfortable. Louisa was not dead—that was a mercy. Louisa had not told of her—that was a good thing, and Louisa must have forgiven her, or she would not have sent her love. Helen could not help owning to herself that the deformed child, whom she had despised so much, was greatly her superior, but she was still too hardened to be contrite. *All will come right at last,* she thought, *Louisa will not tell. When she gets well, I will try and treat her more kindly, for Alice and Mary will be out of the way. I was very stupid to be mastered by my hatred and passion, and may congratulate myself no harm has come out of it, because if Louisa should be ill long, it won't be my fault, for I remember Mother saying that she did not believe the child could live long, she looked so deathly. I'm all right. And now, Miss Helen,* she added, looking in the mirror, *you are well out of this. Take care that your temper does not conquer you again.*

Helen did not humble herself before God, she did not ask Him to forgive her, she did not confess to her heavenly Father that she had sinned against Him, she did not sorrow for her fault. She only rejoiced because her friends did not know, for she did not wish to be condemned by them—she agreed with herself until she became quite cheerful. While Helen thus congratulated herself, her mother entered the room accompanied by the last person in the world that she wished to see—her grandfather, Mr. Holt.

CHAPTER 9

The Two Friends

Betty entered Louisa's room softly, and stood by her little bed for a few moments before the sick child opened her eyes. She could have wept when she saw her flushed face, and uneasy, careworn look, but Mrs. Hall had asked her to be calm for Louisa's sake, and Betty was a brave little woman.

Louisa opened her eyes languidly, and they fell on her companion. She brightened up and said, "Oh, Betty, I wanted so much to see you,

HELEN'S TEMPER

for I am very ill. I don't think I shall live, and I know that I shall be happier in heaven, though I am sorry to leave you and Mother. I'm glad she is better off now, and that I have been able to comfort her, but Sarah is nearly old enough to take my place."

Betty hardly knew how to answer her friend, whom she loved tenderly. She would have liked to cry so much. She stooped over the bed and kissed Louisa fondly, but did not trust her voice to utter one word.

"Betty," continued Louisa, after pausing to

recover her strength, "I want to ask you some questions, and you must promise that you will not tell my mother, nor your mother, what I am going to say. And I wish you, dear, to try and think before you answer me. And, Betty, you will not tell a lie, I know, so that I shall be able to believe everything you say."

Betty's tears did not come now; she was so astonished at Louisa's earnest way of speaking that she wondered what she meant, and forgot for the moment her friend's sick looks in her astonishment. What could Louisa have to tell her that was so particular?

"Betty, before I begin, promise me to be silent."

"I will promise," said Betty.

"The next thing I want you to say is this: 'I will speak the whole truth, Louisa.' Say those words after me." And Betty did as she was told. Louisa turned around in her bed, and looking full into her friend's face, who sat on a low stool at her side, said, "Betty, does your mother think that I make up long stories to excite her pity?"

"No, Louisa, what makes you think so?"

"Never mind. Now, tell me, Betty, do you think I pretend to be good, and am in reality wicked?"

"No, Louisa, I believe you are good, for I know you love Jesus. We can't be wicked if we love Him. At home you are just the same as you are out, and nobody can be wicked who tries to please a father and mother, and be loving to sisters."

"Then you do not think I am a hypocrite, Betty?"

"No, Louisa, I believe you never pretended in your life to be what you were not. Why, even when we first spoke about Jesus, you told me how little you had ever thought about Him. So you see the first day that we met you did not seem to be better than you were."

"Oh, Betty, I am so glad that you believe in me," said the poor child. "It would have broken my heart if you had doubted me. I could not bear that you or your mother should think me good for what I could get."

"But who ever said you were, Louisa?" asked Betty, speaking quickly. "Who would be wicked and cruel enough to think or say such things?"

"Never mind, Betty, I am quite satisfied now. Kiss me, and then read to me just one hymn. I think I could listen to it. Read my favorite, dear, 'A Beautiful Land by Faith I See,' for I seem to see it not so far off, Betty. You will not be sorry for me to die when you think of what my life must have been before I knew you and learned about the Saviour."

"But you have been very happy lately?"

"Yes, dear, I have been much happier, but I always dreaded to walk about because I was so crooked. I fancied every one noticed my back, and that many laughed at me. If it had not been for you on Sunday, I should have been afraid to go alone to Sunday school. I tried so many times not to mind, but it's a thing you can't forget. You can't tell, Betty, what it is to be deformed."

"Louisa, you fancy so much," answered brave little Betty, who felt again so much afraid that she should cry. "You think too much of your lameness and crooked back, and forget that you have a beautiful face and deep blue eyes. You must live, Louisa dear, and I will love you more than ever, and never let you go to Sunday school alone."

Mrs. Hall here interrupted the children, and said that Betty had better not remain any longer. Betty bent over the bed to kiss her friend once more, and Louisa whispered in her ear, "Betty, when you are alone with Helen, tell her I send my love to her, and a kiss, and say that if she would like to see me, I should be very glad indeed to see her."

When Betty reached home, she found her mother and Helen were in the middle of tea, and her grandfather was with them. After the first greeting, Mr. Holt said, "You are soon home, Betty."

"Yes," added her mother. "How did you find Louisa?"

"Oh, Mother!" and the tears that had been forced back so many times fell fast.

"What is it, Betty?" asked her grandfather. "Surely Louisa is not so ill as to make you cry?"

"Yes, yes," said Betty, now sobbing bitterly. "Louisa thinks she is going to die, and wants to go to heaven. And—," here Betty suddenly stopped.

"Go on, little woman," said her grandfather, cheerily.

Betty colored. "Grandfather, I forgot, Louisa made me promise not to repeat what she said to anyone. It would be such a relief to me to tell you and Mother all, for I can't understand her, but I promised not to."

"And you shall not break your promise," said the old man kindly. "I dare say Louisa had good reason for asking you to promise, even though you would have been happier to tell your mother and myself everything."

At this moment Mr. Holt happened to look up, and was struck by Helen's face. She turned red and white in quick succession, and looked so terrified that her grandfather thought as Dr. Brown that there was some mystery to be explained. He took no notice of Helen, but turned to comfort Betty, and expressed a wish to see Louisa, and buy something for her. He asked Betty what she thought the invalid would like best.

"Oh, Grandfather," said the tearful child, brightening up, "there is such a beautiful white rose tree in a pot at Mr. Jackson's, but it costs two shillings, and I have only one. Would that be too much for you?"

"No," answered the kind old man. "I will call for you tomorrow morning early, and we will go and buy it, and take it to Louisa."

Betty jumped for joy. "Thank you, thank you, dear Grandfather! It must make Louisa better, she so longed for a white rose like the one she had in her own garden. And this is far more beautiful than any that ever grew in the open air. Mr. Jackson said it was a greenhouse plant, and that made it so expensive."

When the sisters were alone, Betty gave Louisa's message to Helen. She tossed her head, and thought to herself, *Just like the little beggar to send me a message. She is pretending to be ill. I am not going to be taken in by it.* But she said aloud, "Betty, what did you and Louisa talk about?"

"I dare not tell you," replied Betty.

Helen fancied the *you* was meant to apply especially to herself, and she was more than ever tormented by the longing to know what Louisa had said to Betty, and whether the latter knew her secret.

CHAPTER 10

Grandfather's Present

Betty took a holiday the next day to be with Louisa. She begged so hard to be allowed to take care of her, and as Mrs. Hall was obliged to go out to work, she was thankful to leave Betty in her place. Helen went to school alone, feeling too restless to remain at home. She had been haunted by dreams about Louisa, and had seen her all night long in her dreams, and fancied she could get rid of her miserable feelings at school.

Her mother had been to King's Yard early in the morning to see Louisa, and confirmed the report Betty had given. She thought Louisa was seriously ill, and this opinion had been strengthened by Dr. Brown, who had been to visit the child while Mrs. Smith was there. He told the latter that he had anticipated Louisa's early death, but that some violent shock had worsened her disease. He thought she might linger for some weeks, but in any case he had not expected her to outlive another year, because he had noticed how much weaker she had become during the last few months.

Helen heard her mother repeat the doctor's opinion as she was starting off to school, and she could not help shivering. After all, then, it would be her hand that shortened Louisa's life—her own mad act that hastened the lame girl's death, and she would have to remember it to her dying day. It was a dreadful thought, and Helen quickened her pace, and caught up with some of her schoolfellows, and was glad to chat with them. Anything to make her forget her misery for a time.

Grandfather Holt was not late, as he knew Betty would be waiting for him, and he was almost as anxious to see Louisa as Betty was. He had thought the story of her illness was very mysterious, and there was such a look of guilt about Helen that he was haunted by the remembrance of it all night, and could not divest himself of the idea that his grandchild knew more about the matter than she would confess. On the other hand, he was puzzled to understand in what manner she could be connected with Louisa's illness. Mr. Holt was fully aware of how much Helen disliked the cripple, but he never imagined that her hatred would go beyond words.

Betty and her grandfather were not long in making their purchase. The pot containing the rose tree was wrapped in paper, and Betty carried the present out of the shop. It was a beautiful plant, one or two of the roses were in full blossom, and smelled sweetly, and as the season was late autumn, flowers were scarce. Betty was right, the rose tree had been grown in a greenhouse, and Mr. Jackson said it must be kept in warm air. Betty knew Louisa would take good care of it, and she felt sure that the sight of the roses would put new life into the invalid. Louisa was better, and sitting up in an armchair in the parlor, when Betty and her grandfather entered. Betty ran to her friend and said eagerly, "See, Louisa, what Grandfather has brought to you? He bought it at Mr. Jackson's shop, and would not let me pay half, but said he should like to give it to you for your very own. I am sure you will try and get well now."

Louisa's face beamed with pleasure, though her words were few. She smelled the roses, touched the leaves carefully, and looked at the blossoms as if they were the first she had ever seen.

Mrs. Hall was dressed, ready to go out, and

GRANDFATHER'S PRESENT

said she had only been waiting for Betty to come, and as it was a little past her usual time, she must go to her washing directly. "And

Louisa is so much better," added the happy mother, "that I am not uneasy at having to leave her."

"Do not let me detain you one moment, Mrs. Hall," said Betty's grandfather kindly. "I will spend an hour with Louisa, and help to amuse her, so please go at once."

Mrs. Hall gave a few directions to kind Betty, and then left the room to go and attend to her washing. Mr. Holt sat down by Louisa's side, and asked her how she was.

"Better—much better," answered the little girl. "I am going to try and get well, for everyone wants me to live. I love flowers so much that I am sure these beautiful roses will help me to get strong again."

"Betty," said her grandfather, "I should like you to go and buy a pan for the rose tree to stand in. Then it can be watered, and will not spoil Mrs. Hall's table."

Betty tied on her bonnet, and went away to make her purchase, and the old man was left alone with the sick child. This was just what he wanted.

"Louisa," said Mr. Holt, "tell me all about your fall. How came you to tumble down, dear? Were you running too fast?"

"No, sir."

"Were you walking quietly along?"

"Yes, sir," said Louisa, looking very uncomfortable.

"Did you stumble?"

"No, sir—not that I remember."

"I think I know why you fell, Louisa. You were pushed down."

Louisa's face became many degrees paler, and Mr. Holt feared she would faint. He gave her a little wine, and waited for her to recover herself. *I must learn the whole truth,* he thought, *though I almost feel it is cruel to trouble the child. But for Helen's future well-being I must persevere.*

"Do not think me unkind, Louisa, when I tell you I am determined to find out your secret, and why you have so carefully guarded it. I do so because I believe it is right. But remember, child, I speak in kindness: the girl who pushed you down was Helen Smith."

Louisa clasped her hands in agony, and almost screamed out, "Please, please, sir, don't tell anyone you know about it. Mrs. Smith has been so kind and good to me, and I love Betty so much. But don't tell, please, sir," and Louisa grew so agitated that the old man bent down gently over her and said quietly, "Be calm, my child, and trust me. I will do only what is just. Now tell me why Helen pushed you down, and how it all happened."

"I was going to the grocer's, sir, and we met in a narrow court, and Helen said things to me that were not quite true. And as she left me, she gave me a push, and I fell, sir, and do not remember any more."

"But can you recall the words that Helen said?" asked Mr. Holt. "Think, for a little while, what they were about."

"Oh, please, please, sir, don't ask me."

"Louisa, I must ask you," said the old man gravely. "You tell me that you love Betty. Do you wish her sister Helen to grow up to be a bad woman? Do you not wish her well for your friend's sake?"

"Yes, sir, and therefore I would so much rather not tell you," replied Louisa in a beseeching tone of voice.

"Louisa, I must hear. It is to save Helen that I want to hear. What did she say to you?"

"She doubted my truthfulness, sir, and thought I only pretended to be good for what I could get."

"And so you wanted to ask Betty if she believed in your honesty of purpose?"

"How did you know, sir?" asked Louisa, forgetting that she had wished to conceal the reason why she had enjoined Betty to be silent. "Did Betty tell you?"

"Betty would not break her word. All that she promises you may be sure she will perform," answered Mr. Holt, feeling assured of the truth of his surmises. "Now, Louisa, I have only one or two more questions to ask you. Tell me, why has Helen always disliked you so much?"

"I think, sir, because I am poor and so deformed. Many children laugh at me."

"Because others are so cruel, it does not make Helen's fault less."

"She would not have hated me so much if her fine friends had not found fault with me for going to Sunday school with Betty. They thought I was such a beggar, and Helen considered me not good enough to be her sister's friend. But please, please, sir, don't let Miss Helen know that I have said this to you."

"Louisa, I will promise to do only what is right," said Mr. Holt kindly. "My child, if God sees fit to take you home, are you ready to die?"

"Oh, sir, I hope so, for I do love Jesus. I know how often I act wickedly, but I pray to be better, and the Saviour seems to call me and say, 'Come to me, and you shall find rest.'"

GRANDFATHER'S PRESENT

"Then you are not afraid to die, Louisa?"

"Oh, no, sir. I long to die, for I am often so tired and ill that I hardly know how to move about. In heaven I shall have no pain, and no one will laugh at me for being crooked and lame."

Mr. Holt turned away his head to hide the tears that would come unbidden, and Betty entered most opportunely at this moment with the pan, so that the conversation turned on the pretty rose tree.

Betty's grandfather did not remain much longer. He soon left the happy little girls to themselves. Betty read and sang to Louisa, and then they admired the white roses, and Louisa told the story of the rose tree that stood in the garden of the old home. Betty listened with as much attention as if she had never heard it before, and was enjoying a story that was quite fresh to her.

Chapter 11

Grandfather's Story

"Helen, your grandfather wishes you to go and dine with him," said her mother two days later. "You may come home from school at one o'clock, and then go to your grandfather's house."

Helen did not much care for this arrangement. She dreaded coming in contact with her grandfather; there was something so searching about his looks that she could not face them without feeling uncomfortable. His keen glances abashed her, and made her color—in fact, just then Helen was not at ease with anyone, and lived in perpetual dread of her unkind behavior to Louisa becoming known. And yet she had no intention of going to the latter and confessing her fault, and asking forgiveness.

Helen was growing more familiar with sin. Every hour that she indulged in deceit was leaving its mark on her character. She had never prayed to God since she had pushed Louisa down. She felt she could not do that, for she had conscience enough left to realize the impossibility of such prayer being heard and answered. Alice and Mary were friends with her again, and their influence by no means tended to soften Helen. But for the dark nights, she thought she should not mind, but when the candle was put out, she found thought grew busy, and it took her a long time to fall asleep. When sleep did come at last, she always had Louisa before her in some dreadful

GRANDFATHER'S STORY

form or another. Helen tried to forget that she had behaved cruelly to Louisa, for the latter was getting better, and she was going to be kind to her, and make up with her; that is, if Louisa did not tell on her.

Soon after one o'clock, Helen was seated at dinner with her grandfather, who was purposely alone. He determined to test his granddaughter. He wanted to bring her fault home to her gently and kindly, for he saw that unless some great change took place in Helen's character, she would grow up a bad woman, and bring sorrow to her mother and sisters, for Mr. Holt felt she pretended to be good when her heart was cold and hard.

Helen was somewhat reassured by her grandfather's manner. He was more than usually kind, and made himself so pleasant to her that she forgot her distrust and fears, and was soon chatting merrily to him.

After dinner, Mr. Holt called her to his side, and said, "Now, Helen, I have a story to tell you. Sit down on this stool at my feet, child, and listen to me. All that I am going to talk to you about has happened lately, and I know children always like true stories. There were once two girls, the eldest of them was well behaved, attended Sunday school regularly, and was always so attentive that she could answer any question her teacher put to her. She was constantly at the top of her class, and earned rightful praise for her ability and quickness. All her friends admired her talents, and said, 'What a diligent, well-behaved girl she is. So different from her rough little sister.' The rough little sister was naturally careless and thoughtless, but tried hard to improve. She would sometimes go to school with her lessons unlearned, but was always sorry when she gave pain to her teacher, and she endeavored to correct her many faults.

"As she grew older, she loved Jesus truly, and the more that she knew about Him, the more tender and affectionate she grew to those around her. The world still admired the eldest sister, but those at home loved the little rough child, who was so impulsive, but so real and true at heart. In God's eyes, the well-behaved girl was a hypocrite. She acted entirely to be seen and approved of men, and did not care for the favor and love of her heavenly Father. She was proud in spirit, and did not seek after the meekness and gentleness of Christ. God was not in all her thoughts. Self was her first consideration. Her rough little sister knew what prayer meant. Often in secret she would pour out her heart before God, and confess her many shortcomings in His sight, and entreat the help of His spirit to enable her to conquer herself, and overcome her sins. God heard her prayers—Jesus was near to her, and the angels who frowned at that well-behaved sister smiled kindly on the rough little one and looked forward to the time when she would be gathered into their midst, and form one of their bright company.

"These sisters were returning one day from school, when they met a poor deformed child, one who had suffered much bodily pain from her birth, and on whom the world had pressed heavily.

"She was weeping bitterly, for she had lost her way. She had once known better days, but poverty and disease were her daily portion then. The rough little sister never passed by tears that were evidently flowing from an aching heart. She stopped and ministered to that afflicted one. She led her along the right road, and did not quit her side until she was safe at home. And before she left her, she promised to show her the way to Sunday school, and invited her to come to her class, volunteering to fetch her that day in a week, for it was on a Sunday afternoon when these two first met. The rough little child whom the world did not understand or like, when compared to her more polished sister, led the father and mother of the deformed girl, as well as the latter, to lean on Jesus. She was the instrument in God's hands to bring joy and peace to their poor home.

"All this did not please the polished girl. She hated the deformed child, because she was poor, crippled, ragged, and destitute, and sat at her sister's side in Sunday's class. There came a day when she met the lame child in a narrow court, and having abused her, she —"

"Oh, spare me, spare me, Grandfather, please spare me," cried Helen, whose face had been varying every moment as Mr. Holt's story proceeded. "I see how wrong I have been, how wickedly I have behaved to Louisa."

"You, Helen?" said her grandfather. "I thought you could do no wrong."

"Grandfather, forgive me; you know it all. Oh, please, please, forgive me."

"My child, do not ask forgiveness of me. It is God whose pardon you need to entreat. It is your heavenly Father whom you have offended, and not me. Helen, have you been happier during the last few days that you have gone about with this terrible secret?"

"No, Grandfather, no. I have been trying to get rid of my thoughts, but at night I could not help thinking about Louisa."

"Helen, have you prayed to God since you struck Louisa?"

"No, Grandfather, I could not. But I did not strike her, I only pushed her, and never thought she would fall."

"Whichever you did, the sin was the same. Your jealousy and hatred made you act thus, and see what the end of it will be. Louisa's days are numbered. I have called on Dr. Brown this morning."

"Oh, Grandfather, say that I have not killed her."

"I cannot say that, Helen, for there is no doubt that the fall will hasten her death. At the same time, the doctor says that the disease has rapidly worsened lately. Now, Helen, what are you going to do?"

GRANDFATHER'S STORY

Helen looked up, and repeated her grandfather's words. "What am I going to do? Nothing, for now everyone will know how wicked I have been, and I must bear the shame of it as well as I can."

"Is that all, Helen?"

"What more can I do, Grandfather?"

"Do you wish Louisa to die without seeing her?"

"Grandfather, I have made up my mind to be kind to her when she is better."

"She will never be better, Helen."

"Well, Grandfather, she has forgiven me, for she has sent several messages by Betty."

"Are you satisfied to rest there?"

"What more would you have me do, Grandfather?"

"Let your own heart tell you, Helen."

"Ask God to forgive me?"

"And then Louisa."

"What! That little beggar?" said Helen, her old spirit rising again. "Never, Grandfather. I could not do it."

"Then, child, I have nothing more to say to you," replied Mr. Holt sadly. "You had better have allowed me to finish my story. I had no need to spare you if your spirit is still so obstinate."

Helen looked very much ashamed of herself, and her grandfather saw that a sharp struggle was going on—a fight between good and evil.

"Helen," said the old man solemnly, "if God were to call you hence this night, would you dare to meet Him in this spirit? And how do you know that your life will be spared? Repent, and pray for forgiveness, dear Helen. Oh, do not let your grandfather die, and feel that one in the little circle so dear to him here will be missing at last."

Helen's tears were falling, and she bent her head lower and lower.

"My child, can you join me in prayer now?" asked Mr. Holt, after some minutes of silence.

Helen lifted up her bowed head. "Grandfather,

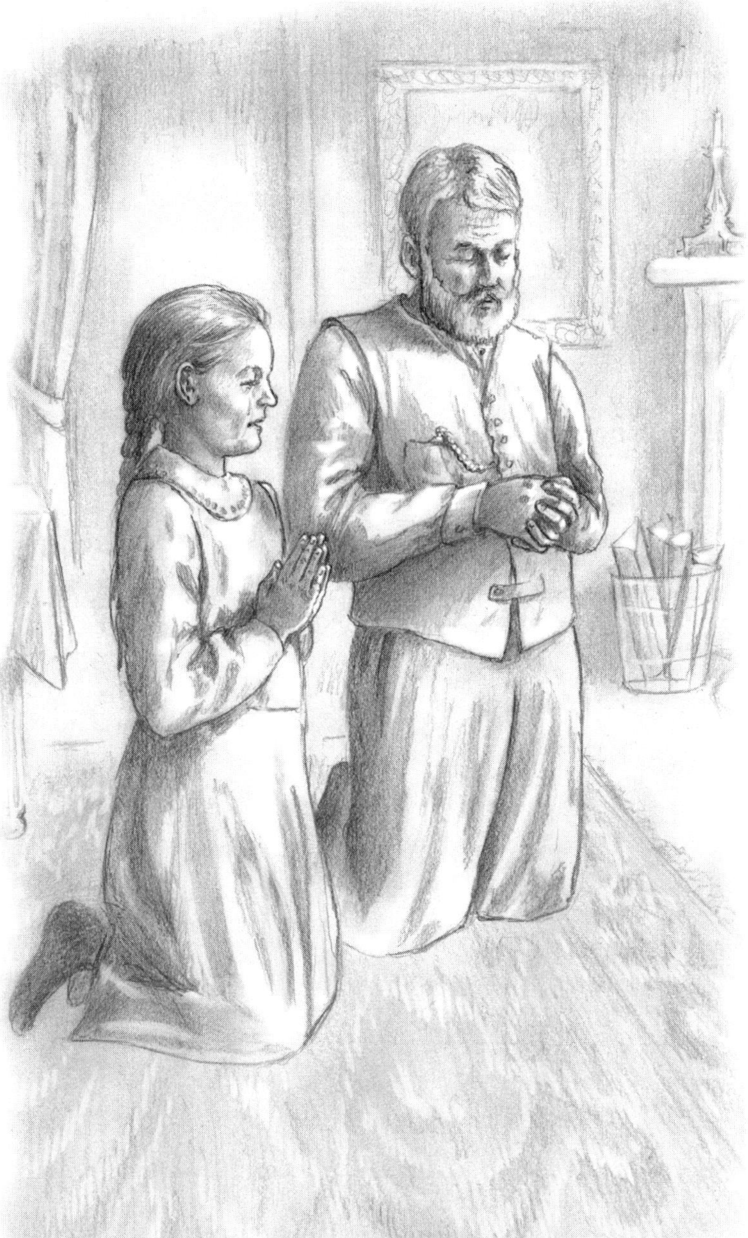

will God forgive me? I have been very wicked."

"We will ask Him, my child."

They knelt, and the gray-haired man of threescore years and ten mingled his tears and prayers with those of his young granddaughter's. Helen rose from her knees softened, and resolved to struggle with her worst nature, God helping her. Helen did not grow suddenly good—there was so much of the old nature to be subdued—but she determined to seek help from Jesus. And she accompanied her grandfather to Louisa's home to ask her forgiveness for the past and tell her of the new future that she hoped would be hers if she made the Gospel of Jesus Christ the rule of her life.

CHAPTER 12

The End

Some weeks after the conversation we have just recorded, a circle of friends were gathered around a deathbed. A child who had had a weary life, suffered much pain, dreaded the laughter and mocking words that often attended her footsteps on earth, had nearly finished her course. Her spirit was hovering between the two worlds, and while her friends were weeping, the angels were rejoicing and waiting for the signal to bear her soul to the bright realms above. There would be no more sin and suffering for her, but there she would sit at the feet of Jesus, who had been so dear to her during the last days of her life.

Her mother sat near to her, holding her hand. Her dearest friend, Betty Smith, was not far away, and another, a little older than Betty, one whom we have known hitherto as a proud, selfish girl, was standing on the other side weeping bitterly as she listened to the words her grandfather Holt had just read, which seemed to bring such peace and comfort to the sick one, Louisa Hall: "They shall hunger no more, neither thirst any more; neither shall the sun light on them, nor any heat. For the Lamb which is in the midst of the throne shall feed them, and shall lead them unto living fountains of waters; and God shall wipe away all tears from their eyes."

Helen has gone through a bitter experience since we last met her. She has watched the life of Louisa gradually fade away, and

THE END

she has known her hand dealt the blow that caused her death. It is true that Mr. and Mrs. Hall have granted her their full forgiveness, and the sick child has welcomed her as a friend, and striven hard to set her mind at rest, and Dr. Brown has said many times that Louisa could not have lived through another winter. All this, and yet Helen cannot forgive the part she has acted. God in Christ has pardoned her—that she feels—but can she pardon herself?

A rose tree stands near to Louisa; its blossoms have lasted just long enough. Never was there a gift that afforded more pleasure to an invalid than this. Its leaves will drop in a few days, and scatter and fade, but not too soon, for before they die, Louisa's spirit will have passed away. The rose tree will be cut down and buried with her. Body and tree will decay in the cold grave, but the most beautiful and godlike part of the deformed child will blossom anew in the kingdom of heaven.

The stillness which followed after Mr. Holt closed the Bible was disturbed by the faint voice of the dying child.

"Helen," said she, "kiss me before I die. You will not forget me, I know, and you will love the dear Saviour more and more every day. Remember that if trouble and difficulties increase, Jesus will be always near."

As Helen bent over Louisa, and kissed her, she murmured, "Oh, Louisa, if it had not been for me, you might have lived on."

"Better, far better to die. I long to go to my Saviour. You don't know, Helen, what a sorrowful life I have lived, though I have tried so hard to be resigned. And since I found Jesus, all has been much brighter. Still, I shall be far better in heaven."

Louisa's words stabbed Helen to the quick. Had not she been one of her greatest torments? Yes, she must reap the bitter fruits of the seed she had so willfully sown.

"Betty, goodbye," said Louisa. "How much I

THE END

owe to you! How kind you have been to me! I shall tell them all in heaven what you have taught me, and you will come up later, when your work is all done here, and join me. Then we shall never be parted again. Mother, do not grieve for me, rejoice that I shall so soon be with my Saviour. Father and sisters, goodbye. Love Jesus. Saviour, I am coming—I am waiting—take me into your arms. Mother, Mother, Jesus is there. He is calling to me. I hear Him say, 'Come to me, little weary one, and I will give you rest.' I am coming."

Louisa stretched out her arms, and with a gentle sigh her spirit passed up to the mansions on high, where aches and pains are unknown, and where sin hath no dominion.

Helen never forgot the great lesson of her life. She lived to a good old age, and many young ones profited by the story of her early years, which she so often repeated. She invariably ended her narrative with these words: "My children, do not forget the true story about myself that I have just related to you, for I have had reason to sorrow bitterly, through a long life, over giving way to my temper, and the sad consequences it produced."

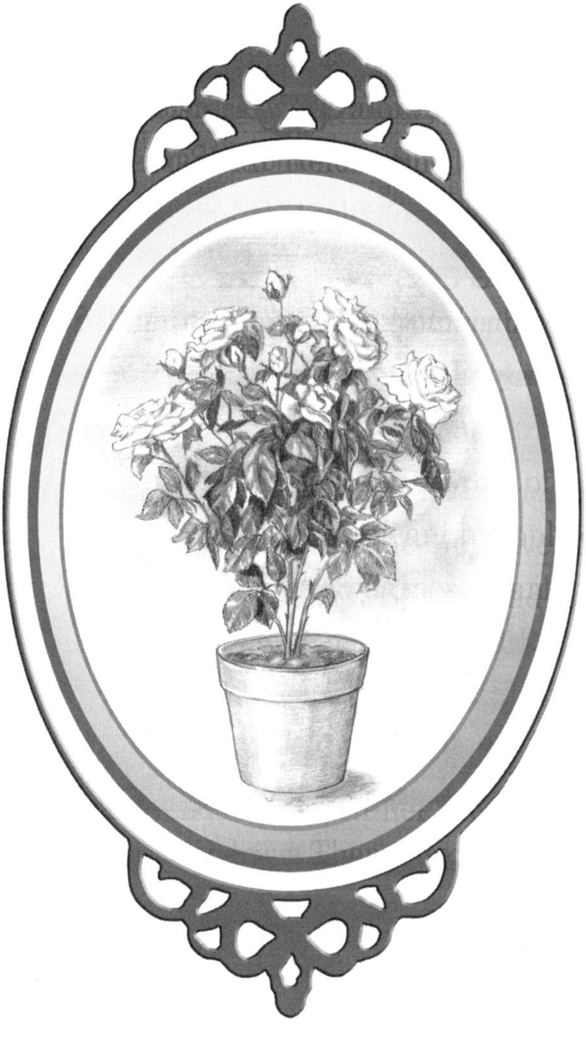

OTHER EARLY CLASSICS
PRINTED BY CHRISTIAN AID MINISTRIES

THE SHEPHERD OF BETHLEHEM
A.L.O.E.

An excellent classic tale originally published in 1877. A small, motley audience listens as a clergyman lectures on the life of David the shepherd-king.

Hardcover | 366 pages | $19.95

THE HERMIT'S CHRISTMAS
DAVID DE FOREST BURRELL

An intriguing story set in the Middle Ages, probably toward the end of the Crusades. As a hermit teaches his visitors the true meaning of Christmas, he is forced to examine his own heart. Originally published in 1912.

Hardcover | 49 pages | $9.99

SOPHY CLAYMORE
A.L.O.E.

A blind orphan girl, adopted by a kind man, flounders in her faith in God. Poverty haunts their footsteps until an unexpected answer turns up, and Sophy learns to trust at last. Originally printed in 1870.

Hardcover | 64 pages | $9.99

NELLY'S DARK DAYS
SARAH SMITH

Young Nelly does not remember her father before he was enslaved in the savage grip of strong drink. Only when he turns to God for deliverance do Nelly's dark days become bright. Originally printed in 1870.

Hardcover | 112 pages | $11.99

THE WOODCUTTER OF GUTECH
W. H. KINGSTON

When the Reformation sweeps across Germany, a woodcutter and his grandchildren hear the story of Jesus' sacrifice on the cross and realize that salvation does not come through performing penances and confessing to the priests. They believe the Gospel and seek to follow God's Word. Read how the woodcutter lives out nonresistance in daily life and through suffering. Originally printed in 1873.

Hardcover | 96 pages | $11.99

SAVED BY LOVE
EMMA LESLIE

Through an orphan friend's love, words, and example, Elfie learns about a loving Father in heaven and is saved from her lonely, wretched existence on the streets of London. Originally printed in 1895.

Hardcover | 136 pages | $12.99

LITTLE AGGIE'S FRESH SNOWDROPS and LITTLE VIOLET
F.M.S.

Follow the snowdrops as they leave the forest at dawn to spread love and cheer to people in need. Journey with a young girl as she turns from self-centeredness to the "law of the violet." Find valuable life lessons in these two tales for the young, originally published in 1871.

Hardcover | 121 pages | $12.99

TOUCHING INCIDENTS
AND REMARKABLE ANSWERS TO PRAYER

Read of the influence of a mother's prayer, how a lame woman was healed, how a father was saved from certain death by his daughter's voice, and much more. Detailed sketches throughout the book. Originally published in 1897.

Hardcover | 347 pages | $15

ROBERT HARDY'S SEVEN DAYS
CHARLES M. SHELDON

Mr. Hardy had one supreme law that he obeyed, and that law was self. Then he had a dream where he saw the Face of Eternity. Convinced that death was imminent, he set out to redeem each of his remaining days. Follow Robert's change of course and be inspired to live each day as your last. Originally printed in 1899. By the author of *In His Steps*.

Softcover | 163 pages | $7.99